THORNHEDGE

ALSO BY T. KINGFISHER

Nettle & Bone

What Moves the Dead

A House With Good Bones

THORN HEDGE

T. Kingfisher

TOR

TOR PUBLISHING GROUP
NEW YORK

THORNHEDGE

Endpaper art and illustrations by Ursula Vernon

A Tor Book
Published by Tom Doherty Associates / Tor Publishing Group
120 Broadway
New York, NY 10271

www.tor-forge.com

Tor® is a registered trademark of Macmillan Publishing Group, LLC.

The Library of Congress Cataloging-in-Publication Data is available upon request.

ISBN 978-1-250-24409-3 (hardcover)
ISBN 978-1-250-24410-9 (ebook)

Our books may be purchased in bulk for promotional, educational, or business use. Please contact your local bookseller or the Macmillan Corporate and Premium Sales Department at 1-800-221-7945, extension 5442, or by email at MacmillanSpecialMarkets@macmillan.com.

First Edition: 2023

Printed in the United States of America

0 9 8 7 6 5 4

THORNHEDGE

CHAPTER 1

In the early days, the wall of thorns had been distressingly obvious. There was simply no way to hide a hedge with thorns like sword blades and stems as thick as a man's thigh. A wall like that invited curiosity and with curiosity came axes, and it was all the fairy could do to keep some of those curious folk from gaining entrance to the tower.

Eventually, though, the brambles had grown up around the edges—blackberry and briar and dog rose, all the weedy opportunists—and that softened the edge of the thorn wall and gave the fairy some breathing room. Roving princes and penniless younger sons had been fascinated by the thorns, which were so obviously there to keep people out. Hardly anybody was interested in a bramble thicket.

It helped, too, that the land around the thorns became inhospitable. It was nothing so obvious as a desert, but wells ran dry practically as soon as they had been dug, and rain passed through the soil as if it were sand instead of loam. That was the fairy's doing, too, though she regretted the necessity.

The fairy was the greenish-tan color of mushroom stems and her skin bruised blue-black, like mushroom flesh. She had a broad, frog-like face and waterweed hair. She was neither beautiful nor made of malice, as many of the Fair Folk are said to be.

Mostly she was fretful and often tired.

"How do they know?" she asked miserably. "Everyone who knew her should be dead of old age by now—them and their children, too! Their *grandchildren* should be gray-haired. How do they even remember there's a tower here?"

She was talking, more or less, to a white wagtail, a little bird that liked short grass and pumped its tail constantly as it walked. Wagtails were not so clever as rooks or jackdaws or carrion crows, but the fairy liked them. They did not make fun of her like the crows would, nor carry tales the way that the rooks did.

The wagtail scurried closer, pumping its tail up and down.

"They must be telling stories," said the fairy hopelessly. "About a princess in a tower and a hedge of thorns to keep the princes out."

She wiped her eyes. She knew that her eyelids were turning blue-black in response to the unshed tears.

There was no one to see her except the wagtail, but she pinched the bridge of her nose and tilted her head back anyway. The old habits were still with her.

"I can't fight stories," she whispered, and a few tears, dark as ink, ran down her face and tangled in her hair.

But time did pass and perhaps the stories were told less often. Fewer men came to the thorn hedge with axes. The wagtails left, because they preferred open country, and the fairy was sorry to see them go. Jays moved in, flitting through the thorns and blistering the air with their scolds. They were shy and spooked easily, for all their cursing. The fairy recognized kindred spirits, as she still spooked easily herself.

As the years trickled away and the thorns filled with dog roses, her soul grew easier. There were stones inside her heart that would never stop grinding together, but they did not weigh so heavily in the years when no princes came.

The fairy was filled with dread when she heard the ringing of nearby axes. She crouched in the brambles, toad-shaped, motionless, thinking, *What will I do if they come nearer?*

But they did not come nearer. They cut a road through the woods but gave the brambles a wide swath. The tower had been built on a rocky hill—a good, defensible place for a castle, but not a good place for a road. The axe bearers cut south instead, in a long curve, over what had once been fields held by the plow.

The fairy was afraid for a long time that the coming of the road would mean the coming of more princes and younger sons, but mostly what it brought were merchants and travelers. None seemed interested in forcing their way through a massive bramble thicket, and perhaps none of them made the connection about how much land the brambles covered, or stopped to wonder what such a dense growth might conceal.

She watched the travelers with interest, for those were the only human faces—save one—that she saw. They were so very different, in so many different shapes and colors. Pale, fair-haired men striding down from the north and dark-skinned men in beautiful armor riding in on horses from the east. Men in caravans who looked like the old royal family, serfs and peasants in homespun, the Traveling Folk in their wagons—a great cross section of humanity who would pass one another on the road and nod and sometimes stop and speak in unfamiliar languages.

(One of the few kind gifts given to and by the Fair Folk is the ability to speak any of the languages of the earth. The fairy could understand what they were saying, but while the words were familiar, the rest was not. She did not recognize the names of the cities they spoke of, nor the kings nor caliphs, and the details of taxation and trade law were beyond her.)

The tide of people grew and grew, and a trade house went up a few miles away. The fairy could see the smoke of it in the sky. She knotted her fingers together and huddled under the thorn hedge to escape the gnawing fear.

"Let them not come," she prayed. She had been told that the Fair Folk were without souls, and probably that applied to her as well, a befuddled creature betwixt and between. Still, just in case, she prayed. "Let them not come here. Let them not clear the thorns. I do not know how many of them I can hold off. *Please* keep them away. Um. Amen."

She added the last worriedly, not sure if that made it a prayer or if she was supposed to be doing something else. The royal family's priest had been reasonably accepting of her presence, but that tolerance had not extended to teaching her how to make a prayer correctly.

Perhaps something heard her prayer. The flow of people slowed to a trickle. The merchants stopped coming. The fairy saw only a few people. There were men in great bird-like masks and dark, tightly fitted clothes that gleamed with wax. They strode by like herons, like birds of prey, and the fairy cowered away from them. There was something about the masks that were too much like the faces of the elder Fair Folk.

Even so, she preferred the bird-men to the screamers. They traveled in groups, half-naked, shrieking like animals. Sometimes they struck themselves with ropes of thorns, howling as the blood flowed, then cackling with laughter. They stank of madness. One ran a little way into the brambles, tearing his skin on the thorns, and then staggered out again.

The fairy, toad-shaped, waited until the rains had come and gone before she came near those brambles again. Whatever madness had infected the screamers, she would not risk contact with it.

After a time, there were neither bird-men nor screamers. There was no one at all. The road filled with weeds.

The fairy, who had been afraid of humans, now began to miss them. Not the screamers or the bird-men, but the others who had come before. They had been company of a sort, even if they did not know she was there.

She slept more and more. The jays stole shiny things from each other's nests but found no new ones.

The seasons chased one another, and a day came when she heard hoofbeats. Men coming from the east, on their fine-boned horses, riding down the ruined road. They wore no armor. There were two bird-men in their midst, also on horses, and they were riding hard as if afraid.

After that, the floodgates opened. Men and women came streaming from the east, and then back from the west, on horses and on foot, in wagons and caravans. Sometimes they rode with knights carrying banners with red crosses on them.

When they spoke to each other, she heard words like *plague* and *graves* and *so many dead*.

The fairy curled into a ball and wept for the dead, and yet a tiny, nagging voice said, *Perhaps the story of the tower will die with them.*

It was a terrible thing to be glad that whole cities had died. *It must be true,* thought the fairy bleakly. *I must not have a soul, to be relieved even a little.* And she cried even more, until the ground was black with tears.

The weeds were trampled down again, in time, and the traffic became more normal. The style of clothing changed and changed again, and the Traveling Folk came again in their wagons, and still no one ventured into the brambles for a long, long time.

It was many years later that a knight came up to the edge of the hedge and stood there, gazing inward. The fairy was broadly aware when people came too near the hedge, with a sensation like a mosquito on her skin. This one stung and she crept toward it, first toad-shaped, then woman-shaped, seeking the source.

She found a campfire, and the knight camped beside it. It was not yet full dark, and he stood with his back to the flame, looking at the brambles.

The fairy did not like that look. It had too much behind it. He was actually looking at the thorn hedge and thinking about it, and that might lead to questions about what was on the other side.

Go away, she thought. *Go away. Quit looking. They can't be telling stories, not now. It's been so long . . .*

Eventually he turned back to the fire. The fairy crept closer.

By the make of his equipment, he was a . . . Saracen? Was that the word? She could not quite remember. But she recognized a knight well enough, whatever his faith.

He was not terribly tall, and his armor was clean but well-worn. His horse had good bones, but the tack was nearly scraped through with cleanliness. The curved sword by his side had empty sockets instead of gems.

It all spoke of genteel poverty, a state that she had come

to associate with younger sons of nobility. The firelight fell kindly but did nothing to dispel the shadows under his eyes, and a well-trimmed beard could not quite hide the hollowness of his cheekbones. Even so, he was probably vastly wealthy compared to her. Toads had little use for coin, which was just as well, because she didn't have any. Even in the days when she had lived within the keep with other people, no one would have thought to pay a fairy.

On the other hand, she could eat worms and beetles and sleep under a stone, which humans could not, so perhaps it balanced out.

He'll leave tomorrow morning, she told herself. *He's searching for a place to camp that won't cost any money—that's all.*

She wrapped her arms around herself. *That's all—*

His head lifted, and for a moment, he was gazing directly at her hiding place.

Her first instinct was to go to toad shape, but that would have meant another motion, even a small one, as she dropped to the earth. Instead, she stayed absolutely still, unmoving, not even drawing breath.

The fire crackled. He looked away.

She exhaled, very slowly, through her mouth. *When his back is turned, toad shape,* she told herself. *And then away. I don't need to see any more. He'll be gone in the morning.*

Eventually he turned to care for his horse, and she dropped to the leaves. The hard, warty toad skin enveloped her, and she hopped slowly away.

He was not gone in the morning.

She was up at dawn, fretting, waiting for him to move on, and he had the unmitigated gall to *sleep in.*

"You're a knight," she grumbled. "Aren't you supposed to be off jousting or toppling citadels for some noble purpose or something?"

Apparently, he was getting a late start on the citadel. The morning was half-over before he rose, and it was nearly noon before he had finished mending a stray bit of bridle and finally saddled his horse.

And then he didn't get on it. He took it by the reins and *walked.*

She trailed at a distance, waiting for him to head to the road.

He didn't.

He walked along the edge of the brambles, always looking inward, skirting the areas where the briars grew thickly in the hollows. On one particular rise, where the hedge of brambles was thin, he stopped.

He dropped his horse's reins over its head, ground tying it, and then prowled in front of the hedge. *Looking.*

The fairy could have screamed.

She took shelter under a fallen log farther down the slope and watched him watching the wall.

What's he searching for? Is he trying to find a way in?

She found herself gazing past him at the thorn wall, trying to imagine what he was seeing. Surely there was nothing there to hint at the tower inside—the roof had been pulled off by the briars long ago, and what remained was cloaked in trees. It looked like a tall thicket on a hillside, surrounded by a bramble patch.

If you looked in exactly the right place, you might see a few lines a little too straight to be a tree trunk—but you had to know exactly where to look.

He can't see that. I can barely see it, and I remember when the tower was new. Oh, why won't he go away?

He did not go away. He led his horse onward, making a slow circuit of the thorn hedge. The fairy followed.

By the time evening came, he had returned to his original campsite. He set his horse to graze and built up the fire again.

If he doesn't leave on his own, she thought, *I will have to drive him off. Spook his horse. Tie elf-knots in his hair. Something.*

He turned and glanced up at the sky, orange light painting the side of his face. He did not look like a man who would be easily driven away by elf-knots.

I could turn into a toad at him. Or . . . um . . .

She raked her hands through her hair. She had so few powers, and the ones she had were mostly tied up inside what was left of the tower. Now . . . well, she could call up fish. Fish would probably not help the situation. She could try to talk a kelpie into helping her, but they were wild, and anyway, she would have to go somewhere that had kelpies, and that would involve leaving the keep unguarded.

I will start with elf-knots, she told herself firmly. *Lots and lots of them. It will take him a week to comb his hair.*

When he had banked the fire and settled down, when his breathing had become slow and even, she slunk into the open. She would have felt safer in toad shape, but elf-knots required fingers.

The campsite was full of deep blue shadows. A true fairy—one of the Fair Folk by birth and blood—could have folded themselves into the smallest of those shadows and become as invisible as a spiderweb.

She was not so gifted. She could only go quietly, setting her bare feet where there were no twigs or leaves to give her away.

The knight did not move. His hands were curled neatly beside his head.

She crouched over him, the least likely of predators, and listened to his breathing.

When several minutes had passed without movement, she gave a soundless sigh and her shoulders slumped with relief.

He had thick, curly hair—the perfect sort of thing for elf-knots. The fairy stretched out her fingers and touched a single strand.

It flexed and shivered, slowly teasing away from its companions. She frowned with concentration.

Like an impossibly slender serpent, the hair began to move on its own. It tangled around the lock of hair closest to it, doubled back on itself, tangled again.

She flicked her fingers again and a second hair joined the first, then a third. They snaked in and out, drawing others with them.

Half knot, half braid, the resulting knot grew larger, binding together dozens of individual hairs, then hundreds.

When a section of his hair as thick as her thumb was a solid mat, she sat back on her heels and let out her breath.

It's been so long. But I always was good at elf-knots—

His hand closed gently over her wrist.

"Are you quite done?" asked the knight.

CHAPTER 2

The fairy stared down at the hand on her wrist, and her thought was not that she was caught, but that someone was touching her.

It had been many years since a living being had touched her. She could not remember how many years. She had almost forgotten that such things were possible—and yet there it was, the solid weight of a palm and four fingers pressed against the underside of her wrist.

"I was going to ask if you were one of the djinn," said the knight slowly, sitting up. "But they are made of fire, and there is no fire in you."

She shook her head, still staring at his hand. Her skin looked green and sickly in the moonlight next to his.

"Are you an elf, then?"

It seemed important not to lie. She licked her lips and said, "Something like an elf. Yes."

"I see."

She had spoken to him, and he had spoken back. That also had not happened for many years.

He released her wrist. She looked up, startled.

He made a little half bow, more of a nod, still seated. "You have been following me," he said. "I thought you were something more malign. I did not mean to frighten you."

His face was serious and polite. The mat dangling by his left ear looked ridiculous.

He was talking to her.

"I was—" The fairy had to stop, as the absurdity of speaking to a person and having them speak back nearly overwhelmed her. If she thought about it for too long, she would start laughing or crying or both. "I wasn't frightened."

It occurred to her that she could run away. He was sitting and she was crouched, and she had a good chance of making it to the trees. Once she was in toad shape, she could hide in the leaves.

I should go. I will go.

She did not move.

"Why were you following me?" he asked.

She thought about this. She did not dare tell him all the truth. "This is my place," she said finally. "You are in it."

"I apologize for my trespass, madam."

He moved then, holding up his hands, away from her. "I am going to build up the fire," he said. "Please stay."

No one had asked her to do anything since before the tower fell. She took a half-hearted step toward the woods, then stopped. The skin on her wrist rang like an echo.

He laid a log on the fire and stirred it until it crackled. Then he sat down and looked across it at her.

"Does the fire trouble you?" he asked. "Can you sit beside it?"

Troubled by the fire? What manner of creature does he think I am?

Still, perhaps it was not that strange a question. She never lit fires herself. When it was cold or damp, it was easier to take toad shape. Toads were not particularly bothered by damp, and they sank into a peaceful torpor in winter, beneath the leaves.

She came a little closer, keeping the fire between them. He had asked her to stay, and so she would for a little while, but if he made any move to catch her, she would run.

The silence grew awkward. She lifted her hands to her temples. "Forgive me," she said. "It has been . . . I have not had to talk to anyone . . . It has been a long time." She grimaced. "Are you a . . ." She tried to find the right word from among the half dozen her gift offered. "Saracen?"

His eyebrows shot up. He looked briefly offended, then his face smoothed. "It has been a very long time, I expect," he said. "That word is not used much anymore."

I've said something wrong. That didn't take long. She flushed. "I'm sorry."

He shook his head. "It is all right. How long *have* you been here?"

Wanting to hurry past the moment, she was more honest than she meant to be. "I don't know. Years. I kept meaning to count the winters, but I would sleep and then I couldn't remember how many I had forgotten." She made a vague gesture with one hand, toward the road. "Before people built that."

His eyebrows went up again.

"There were a lot of people," she said. She could not seem to stop talking, now that she had started. There was some enormous store of words bottled up inside her, it seemed. "Then very strange people, then no one. Then more people again who looked like you, talking about the plague—"

The knight rubbed a hand over his face. "You have been here since before the Death," he said. "God have mercy."

That seemed a very strange thing to say, but the fairy did not want to risk being wrong again. She clasped her hands together and asked, very carefully, "What do you mean by the Death?"

"A great plague," he said. "Justinian's third plague. It killed half the world, they say. Perhaps a little less. In the Holy Land, though, they found a cure, and they brought it north to heal those who were left. But so many had died and all the fields were lying fallow." He held his hands out, palm up. "There are songs about it now. My people came from Anatolia in the east, fleeing a great famine, and they came here and found all this land and hardly anyone left to work it. Of course, nobody wanted their land taken by outsiders, but they also didn't want it going to weeds and wilderness, and the lords that survived were handing out property left and right, because they'd lost so many serfs, you see. And then the Seljuks were fighting Byzantium and whoever won, they were likely to come calling here next, so there was a land act, I think—maybe two?—and a few minor squabbles over who was in charge of what was left, and then I think the Danes got involved somehow . . . I'm sorry, I can't remember all of it, or the order it goes in. I might have part of it backward. I like books, but I can't memorize dates the way some people can."

She nodded. It all seemed very strange. Half the world dead? Was that possible?

She stared at the fire, thinking of how many people that must be, all of them real, and how she would never be able to hold them all in her head or mourn for each of them. She hoped that there had been someone to mourn properly for them. She did not think she could take on another task and hope to see it done.

"Do elves tell their names to mortals?" asked the knight.

The great Fair Folk did not, but since the fairy had no true name for someone to use against her, it hardly mattered. "Toadling," she said.

He frowned at her. "It does not seem kind to call you that."

It was her turn to frown. Had she said something wrong again? No, she had been Toadling for her whole life. The greenteeth had given her the name when she was barely born.

"Toadling," she said firmly. "It is what I am called."

"And I am Halim," he said. "And I apologize for trespassing in your forest."

Toadling considered this. "It is all right," she said, "so long as you leave again."

She felt an odd hitch in her chest as she said it. It had been so long since she had spoken to another person, and she had not come even close to using all the words that she had stored up. She did not want him to leave. She did not want him to stay. She put her hands up to her face.

Halim frowned. "I do not wish to offend you," he said, "but I cannot leave just yet. There is something here that I wish to see."

Toadling looked up at his face, startled.

"There is *nothing* here," she said. Her voice was high and it sounded angry, and Toadling, who had always hated any kind of conflict, wanted to recoil from it immediately. "Nothing!"

"There is at least one thing here," said Halim, smiling faintly. "A fairy girl that I am looking at right now. That is something."

Toadling shook her head angrily. "Nothing important," she said. "You should leave. There is nothing here."

"If there is nothing here, then why does it matter if I leave?" he asked.

She inhaled sharply, and he held up both hands. "I am sorry," he said. "That was unkind. You have asked me to leave, and it is hardly the act of a good knight or a good Muslim to stay against a lady's wishes."

A lady. Toadling wanted to laugh, but if she started, she would never stop and it would turn to crying almost immediately, she was sure, and everything was already terrible, and that would only make it worse.

"There is a story," Halim said, watching her closely, "of a beautiful maiden in a tower, enchanted by some terrible magic."

"There cannot be a story," said Toadling, almost inaudibly. "Everyone has been dead for so long. There cannot be a story. Who told you such a story?"

She took a deep breath, aware that she had not denied it strongly enough. "There is no tower," she said. "And no maiden. I tell you, there is nothing here."

"Then why are you here?" asked Halim.

She was silent too long, she knew, before she said, "I live here."

"Are you the enchanted maiden?" asked Halim.

Toadling stared at him, and this time, she did begin to laugh.

She tried to choke it off, but she had been right. She kept laughing and it was a horrible barking laugh, like a toad croaking, and then there were black tears on her cheeks.

She heard Halim move and could not bear to look at his face. It would be horror or pity, and she wanted neither. She dropped into toad shape, not caring how it looked, and heard him swear.

At least the change had stopped her laughing. Toads are capable of sarcasm, but their blood runs too cold for hysteria. She scrambled into the leaf litter and away.

He was still there in the morning. Toadling lurked under a log near his campsite, waiting for him to do . . . something.

She had relived their conversation in her head a hundred times over the course of the night and come to the conclusion that she had been foolish. She should have laughed when he said there were stories—laughed and then stopped laughing. If she could not laugh, she should have been grave and serious and told him that he had been misled.

I should have done anything other than what I did. I am a fool and more than a fool.

What remained to be seen was whether he would leave on his own, or whether more words would be required to fix the mess that she had made by speaking in the first place.

She hoped not. *It has been too long. I have forgotten how to make words do what I wish.*

He did not leave. Instead, he carefully dressed, boiled tea, and then rose to his feet.

He walked to the edge of the woods and cleared his throat.

"Mistress Toadling, I wish to apologize. I spoke poorly to you last night, and I regret it."

He was facing away from her and clearly had no idea where she was. Toadling lifted a back leg and scratched the side of her head.

"I particularly should not have cursed. I am sorry. It was unworthy of me. I know that my presence here is unwelcome, and my wish is not to impose."

He turned partway, running a hand through his hair. She noted that he had cut out the mass of elf-knots.

"Please, Mistress Toadling, you owe me nothing, but I would be grateful if you would speak to me again."

In profile, his face was almost handsome and very grave. He stood for a moment with his lips pressed together, resolute, and then ruined the effect completely by sighing and muttering, "*Dammit.* I don't even know if she's listening."

Toadling surprised herself by standing up, shedding her toad skin, and saying, "I'm listening."

Halim jumped but composed himself quickly, she'd give him that. "Mistress Toadling!"

He inclined his head politely, though even that was more courtesy than Toadling was used to. She rubbed the back of her neck.

"I am sorry," he said again. "I have handled this very badly from first to last. I began by laying hands on you and then by arguing with you. I am not the best of knights."

Toadling shrugged. "Will you leave?" she asked.

Halim frowned. "I am not sure I should," he said.

This was not the answer that she was expecting. She clasped her hands together. "You should," she said. "You most certainly should. There is no reason for you to stay."

Halim sat down beside the fire. After a moment, Toadling crouched on her heels on the other side.

"I have come because of a story," he said. "You were right that everyone who might have told it is dead. I read it in a book. Several books."

Toadling felt her stomach drop. *Books.*

Books were terribly expensive. Surely . . . surely no one would have thought that her father's kingdom was important enough to write down in a book.

She clutched her temples. "Where did you read such a book?" she asked. "Who would have written it down? I cannot believe . . ."

She was supposed to be saying that there was no tower. She was failing at this again. He had surprised her, and she could not think fast enough. She had been a toad too long; her blood was sluggish with it . . .

"It was an old book," he admitted, "where I found it first. It named a kingdom that I had never heard of, and I was half-mad with boredom and looking for something to do." He smiled faintly. "There is not a great deal of use for younger sons of poor noble families, you know. My mother thought I might become an alim, but I had no inclination at all, and so I was an overeducated young knight who could barely afford his own arms and armor."

"I did not know that . . . ah . . ." Toadling tried to think of a word that was not *Saracen*. "That . . . Mussulmen? . . . Became knights."

"Muslim," said Halim. "And not a terribly devout one, if you must know. My mother was devout enough for the whole family, so we left her to it." He poked at the fire. "It has been over two hundred years since the plague, mistress. I suspect you would find the world very different now."

Two hundred years!

It was immense—unthinkable—and ultimately meant nothing at all.

Two years or two hundred or two thousand. The magic endures. Toadling sighed.

"It does not matter," she said. "I will not be going out in it, so long as it leaves my little wood alone."

It was Halim's turn to sigh. "The world rarely leaves anyone alone," he said. He poked at the fire again. "Well. In answer to your question, you will find that there are Muslims and Christians and people who have gone back to the old gods, and an order of knights for each of them. Being a knight isn't about being religious, you know, so much as it is to figure out what to do with your extra sons so they don't tear up the family seat. Every now and then someone gets the idea we should start chopping each other's heads off, but in practice, the Pope squats in Rome like a spider and the caliphs glare at one another over their walls, and the rest of us get along as best we can with each other." He smiled faintly. "I found the references to the tower and the princess in the library of a Benedictine monastery, in fact. The Brother Librarian was a good man and glad of someone to talk to."

Toadling shook her head, dismayed. That the world had changed did not surprise her, but that somewhere a monastery had a book with the story of the tower in it . . .

"It was not true," she said, but her voice sounded unconvincing even to herself.

"There was a stone keep here," Halim said. "Five or six hundred years ago, at least. I found it in the old land records. And I have ridden over the country for forty leagues in every direction, and the only place that it could have been is—there."

He pointed into the woods, directly at the hidden tower. Toadling tried not to flinch.

"Now," he said, when it became obvious that she was not going to say any more, "it is possible that the story was false, and there was never a maiden in the tower and never a wall of thorns. It is a good story, and perhaps whoever wrote it down simply put the name of an old castle to it, to make it seem more realistic."

Toadling twined her fingers together. She felt like he was setting a trap, and anything she said was going to set it off.

"My brothers would say that I am being very foolish, wasting my time on stories," said Halim. "They would tell me to work on my swordplay instead, so that I can finally win a tourney. But I do not particularly enjoy tourneys, and I do like stories. And I would still like to get into that old keep, if God wills it, and see if there is a tower. Perhaps there is no maiden sleeping in it after all. But there is a great deal of magic in the world, and I will not dismiss the possibility."

"There is no maiden," said Toadling. "Your brothers were right."

Halim put his chin in his hand. "Perhaps you are the enchanter," he said.

Toadling went very still.

"Or if you aren't the enchanter, you might be enchanted yourself. Should I be trying to break the curse on you?"

Toadling blinked at him, aware that she was goggling like a startled frog. "*What?*"

"Is there a curse on you?" he asked, leaning forward. "Oh my! Is that it?"

"No . . . ?" The conversation was moving too fast for her again. "I'm not cursed!"

"Which is exactly what you'd say if you were," he pointed out.

"But it's exactly what I'd say if I wasn't!"

"Well, that's true." He considered. "Suppose that I go inside the keep and look around. If you're cursed, maybe I'll figure out how to break it, and if not, then I'll leave you in peace."

"I'd rather you just left!" she said. "You won't find anything inside!"

He pounced on that. "So there *is* a keep, then!"

Toadling opened her mouth, closed it, then let out a single furious sob.

His grin of triumph died instantly. He made a move toward her, then stopped himself. "Mistress Toadling—gah. I did not mean to cause you pain. I talk too much. I'm sorry."

Apologies made it worse. She had long experience with unkindness, but apologies undid her. Her eyes prickled and she dashed blue-black tears away. Her face would look as if she had been beaten again. *Damn.*

"Go away," she said miserably. "Go away, go away! You're only going to make a mess of things!"

She put her face in her hands. A moment later, there was a pressure on her shoulder, and it occurred to her that he had put a hand there, very lightly.

"Please don't cry," he said. "I'm sorry. If I go, will you come with me?"

Toadling stared up at him. She knew that her face was a mask of ink, but for a moment she was too surprised to care. "Come with you? Where?"

"Anywhere you like," he said. "You've been here a long time. The world is different. It might be better. You could see for yourself."

Leave? Leave here?

For a moment, she wanted it so badly that she could taste it.

No. No. I can't go. If I go, even if it gets him away, even if I can somehow keep the spell up from a distance, sooner or later there will be another prince, another knight, someone who reads that book . . . Someone will come.

And if they get inside, she can get out.

"I can't," she whispered.

"Why not?" he asked. "There are so many things to see. If you don't trust me—and who can blame you?—I will take you to my mother. She'll be a little surprised to have an elf about the house, but she is the kindest woman imaginable."

"I can't." She shook her head. "Not won't. *Can't.* I would, but I can't leave. I—I'm sorry."

"Is there some magic that keeps you here?" he asked. He patted her shoulder very carefully.

"Yes," she said, grateful for the out. "That's . . . that's the best way to explain it. Your offer is very kind. I wish I could take you up on it. Truly. But I can't."

Halim nodded. "In that case," he said, taking his hand away and giving her an odd little half bow, "then, Mistress Toadling, I will go."

She sagged, partly with relief, partly with disappointment. The moment caught in her throat like pain.

"And I will return," said Halim, "before too much longer, and find a way to free you from that magic."

A fter he left, Toadling found herself at loose ends.
She did not miss the strange knight, exactly. To miss someone, or not miss them, seemed to require that there be some relationship beyond two brief meetings. She had more right to miss the wagtails that had once run across the grass around the tower.

It was more as if time had divided itself in half around him, falling into two separate pieces—the time before she spoke to him, and the time after.

Normally, when she took on toad skin, she also took on toad thoughts and spent her days in contemplation of nothing more complicated than earthworms and millipedes moving under the leaves. Time would pass over her head and she would hardly notice, unless some human activity required human thoughts.

Now, however . . . now she found herself thinking un-toad-like thoughts. She would snap up a fat worm and think in the next instant about leaving, about hopping to the edge of the road and taking on human form and simply walking *away.*

Which was madness. Which she could not do.

"This is ridiculous," Toadling muttered to herself, taking human form again—and she was muttering out loud again, a habit that she thought she had shed long ago. "This is absurd. The worms won't be different anywhere else. He spoke to me for a few moments. He stayed for two days. Why am I still thinking about this?"

Nevertheless, she was. She worried at the memory in her head, the words she had said, the ones she hadn't said, the ones that she should not have said at all.

Half the world had died of the plague and made less impact on her than a few moments of conversation.

After a week—was it a week? She had gotten out of the habit of marking time. It seemed like a long time, but only because she was thinking so much—she came to a decision.

"I should check," she said. "I should make sure. In case . . . in case something has happened."

(She did not even dare think to herself that the sleeper might be dead. The relief might kill her if it were true.)

For the first time in many years, Toadling entered the keep.

In the beginning, she had visited the keep daily, to reassure herself that the sleeper was still there. Then, slowly, the need to check had faded. She had gone back every few weeks, then once a year, then not at all.

It was easier that way. The sleeper became restless if she visited too often.

The thorn hedge, which was so inaccessible to a human, was far different when one was the size of a toad. The brambles became a series of highways, pounded down by the feet of mice and the long bodies of snakes.

Toadling hopped through the thorn hedge. The thorns were as large as roof timbers to a toad, and as easily avoided. She reached the stones of the keep itself and slipped easily through a drainage hole. The far end was plugged with wet leaves, but nothing she could not force her way through.

The walls around the central courtyard were still standing. The thorns had pulled a few stones from the walls, but that was all. It was the south tower where the plants had concentrated, sending long whips up the walls and covering it in a riot of green.

She stood up, out of toad shape, and walked the courtyard. Her fingers trailed over moss and lichen. Trees grew thickly inside the walls, a small unlikely forest.

The main hall had lost its roof long ago, and an oak tree had grown up inside it. Toadling had no interest in it, or in the squat north tower. If she walked there, she risked waking too many memories.

She went to the base of the south tower and stood, looking up.

The magic was concentrated near the top of the remains of the tower, but she could feel it from here. It was like stepping into a warm rain. Individual droplets of magic beaded invisibly against her skin, and she brushed them away with her hands.

It was her own magic, but it had been separated from her for so long that it felt unfamiliar, like returning to a childhood nursery when one was grown.

A skilled climber might have been able to get up the outside of the tower, but that was a long, difficult way. Instead, Toadling pulled herself up to one of the narrow windows, took toad shape again, and slipped inside.

The interior was dark. She felt her way up the steps on human hands and knees. The magic was stronger here—witness the fact that the steps had not fallen apart over the centuries—and she had to wipe it away from her face as she climbed.

The drops became a stream, became a torrent, and then Toadling was swimming in the magic, surrounded by it.

She came to the landing at the top of the tower.

The doorway was open. The door had been torn off its hinges, and Toadling did not have the skill to replace it. The roof was gone, but the vines clustered so thickly overhead that they made a ceiling the color of knotted veins.

Dried leaves crunched under her feet as she entered the bedroom.

And there she was, curled up on the bed. Her golden hair fanned out around her. Her chest rose and fell, and she had a slight smile on her lips.

Toadling stood over the maiden that she had enchanted and let out a long, long sigh.

CHAPTER 3

Toadling had been taken by the fairies less than an hour after she was born.

There were many precautions in those days for keeping changelings at bay. Bits of cold iron tucked into the blankets, a lodestone hung above the cradle, three rowan twigs wrapped in red thread and tucked under the pillow. But Toadling's mother was bleeding heavily and her ladies swarmed around her, and Toadling was set down in the cradle without any wards at all.

By the time the bleeding had stopped, there was a changeling in the crib, and Toadling had been taken into Faerie.

It is true that sometimes the fairies steal human children for themselves, but Toadling was not one of them. The goal of the thieves was to leave a changeling in the crib, and what became of Toadling afterward was of no concern to them.

There are a great many things that can happen to an infant in Faerie, and most of them are bad.

Toadling was, more or less, lucky. She was not harvested by the flesh-smiths nor devoured by redcaps, nor raised in the retinue of a great lord of Faerie.

Instead, she was thrown to the greenteeth, the slimy swamp-dwelling spirits who devour unwary swimmers.

Boy-children they eat, always. Girl-children they eat, mostly.

But occasionally their numbers will fall, or one of them will be seized with some murky maternal instinct, and they will raise a child instead.

The greenteeth gave her the name Toadling. If she had swallowed a mouthful of mother's milk before the fairies took her, things might have been very different. But the first food she ate was a slurry of fish and pondweed, and by the magic of the greenteeth, she did not die of it.

Because she had eaten no human food, because she was barely born, Toadling's flesh was malleable to magic. The greenteeth were able to teach her how to lie unmoving in the cold water, with only her eyes above the surface. She could not quite breathe water, but she could hold her breath for many minutes, and she would lie at the bottom of the stream, picking up shiny stones and tickling the bellies of passing fish.

At night—or what passed for night in Faerie—the greenteeth slept in a tangle of long, bony limbs and waterweed hair. The oldest of them held Toadling, cradling her with her face just above the surface of the water, and she fell asleep with the sound of frogs croaking in her ears.

When she was about nine years old, as humans would judge it, she learned the trick of toad shape. One of the younger greenteeth taught her, a swollen-bodied, spindly-limbed sprite called Duckwight. Duckwight was hideous and her teeth were the color of moss, but she was as patient as water flowing over stone.

They practiced for weeks, holding hands. They stood up, they squatted down, over and over, with Duckwight's magic flowing over them both.

At first, Toadling could not quite understand what was happening, and then she began to feel the magic, like water building up behind an earthen dam. It was a trickle, not a torrent, but it grew and grew, and one day, without even realizing how it happened, the magic split into two streams, the dam broke, and Toadling dropped down into another shape entirely.

Duckwight clapped her webbed hands together and squalled with delight. The other greenteeth swarmed around them, patting Toadling and praising her. She did the trick for them again and again, and the greenteeth slapped their bony hands together and called her by the name that she would bear for the rest of her life.

Surrounded by child-eating swamp spirits, Toadling felt intensely loved.

S he was fifteen when the hare goddess came for her.

The goddess had fur tipped with moonlight and eyes as deep as wells. She came running over the hills, stretching out her long legs, and stopped on the bank of the river.

There were three of them in the water—the Eldest, Duckwight, and Toadling. The Eldest swam to the edge of the bank and bowed deeply to the silver hare. Duckwight took Toadling's hand and drew her to the bank, but the grasp of her webbed fingers was tight and frightened.

"Goddess," said the Eldest, in the screaming language of the greenteeth.

The goddess dipped her head in acknowledgment. "Younger sister," she said. "I have need of your foundling."

Duckwight cried out in sudden grief and hid her face behind her hair.

"She is one of us," said the Eldest. It was not a denial of the goddess, only a statement. "In a hundred years, no one will know that she was not born among the waters."

"Then I have come in time," said the goddess. "I must take her now."

"I don't want to leave," said Toadling, realizing what was happening. She swallowed. The word *foundling* had reached down into her heart and made a sound that she did not like.

"And I do not want to drag you away," said the great silver hare, turning her liquid eyes on Toadling. "But we are not always given the choices that we want."

Duckwight moaned and clasped Toadling to her. Her waterweed hair tangled around them both.

The Eldest waited for a few moments, then gently pulled Toadling away. Duckwight sobbed black tears into her hands.

The ancient greenteeth was the oldest of her kind, but her teeth were sharp as razors. She bit Toadling's left palm, across the heel of her hand, and left a semicircle of tooth marks.

"Remember us," she said, picking up a handful of river mud and laying it over the wound. "Remember us, and if you can, find your way back to us in time."

Toadling nodded. Tears were forming in the corners of her eyes and running over her skin, and the bite on her hand smarted under the healing mud.

The silver hare took Toadling up on her back. There was no other word for it—Toadling was fairly certain that she had not climbed up on her own. But suddenly she was astride the broad, furry back and moonlight was pooling up against her skin.

The hare nodded to the Eldest, touched Duckwight with her nose, and then turned and dashed away.

It was not like riding a horse—not that Toadling had ever seen a horse. But she had ridden the shining black kelpies that lurk on the riverbanks, and this was not at all like that. It was more like lying in a meadow that happened to be moving at extraordinary speed.

The hare ran across the fields of Faerie, with Toadling lying flat against her back, and things passed long and wordless between them.

She would never be able to describe the ride. No one ever asked her, but she would have liked to have the words to fit around it, if only for herself. It was like a dream that went on for many hours, and in the morning the fragments still lay dusted across her shoulders.

When they arrived at last at a tall tower, Toadling knew enough to slip down from the goddess's back. Her bare feet made no sound on the cobblestones.

"Here," said the hare, her eyes glowing silver. "Here you stay, and learn what you can. Your father's house will have need of you in time."

Toadling stared at her palm, at the scabbed line of tooth marks.

"What do I care for my father's house?" she asked. It was a tiny rebellion, but it was the first one she had ever uttered.

The hare flicked her ears. "Nothing," she said. "Nor may you ever. Nor do I. But I do not like suffering and will stop it where I can, and for that you must help me. These people will teach you what you may need to know."

She dashed away again. The earth should have rung like a bell under her footfalls, but somehow it did not.

Toadling turned.

She was in a courtyard. A man was approaching her, holding a lantern. He had a face like a catfish and the hair that sprouted from his ears moved restlessly, like whiskers.

"I see," he said. "I see. I am Master Gourami, and we will begin your schooling here."

Toadling's schooling could have gone a great deal better, and the only consolation, perhaps, is that it could have gone a great deal worse.

It was a tiny backwater of the fairy court, but for Toadling it was overwhelming.

She was not ignorant. She knew the true names of every plant that grew within a thousand feet of the river and how to coax them into growth. She knew how to address a grindylow, if one swam up from the grim depths of the lake, and she knew the conflicted hearts of kelpies and how to soothe one when it ran mad.

She could recite every song and story of the greenteeth, braiding them together and unwinding them over the course of a night. She could start a balefire of fish bones and see a tiny piece of the future in the way the spine cracked apart.

In the fairy court, these things were useless, and so she was considered stupid.

She left the greenteeth knowing everything worth knowing about her world and came to the fairy court to find that she knew nothing at all.

Toadling had never worn clothing. She had never gone into a tiny room to squat on a board to relieve herself. The taste of cooked food was strange on her tongue, and beds were strange, hard things compared to the embrace of water.

The hardness of the bed was the least of it, however. Toadling had never slept alone. The greenteeth piled together under the water, mostly in a heap. Sometimes, if one was restless, she would move a little way off, but never far enough that she could not hear the sounds of the other greenteeth breathing underwater.

The first night, in the strange room, Master Gourami pointed to the bed and explained that people slept on them. (It did not occur to him to explain about the blankets, but that did not matter, because Toadling did not mind the cold.)

And then he went out and shut the door behind him, and the first lesson that Toadling learned, in that strange place, was loneliness.

It took her a year to learn to read, and she was never easy with it. The greenteeth had a way of using their necklaces, each bead waking a memory, and that was a little like reading, so the concept was not completely foreign to her. Toadling dreamed sometimes of Duckwight's webbed fingers stringing letters together one after another. Each word called up would summon a torrent of memories, so much of Toadling's trouble was in concentrating on the present. Every time she read *stone,* her mind wanted to pull up the round pebbles underneath the river and the mossy overhangs of the banks and the cold flagstones of the courtyard and the gray stone with the hole in it that the Eldest had dangled in front of her as an infant.

She would be left sitting for many minutes, staring at the single word on the page, while memories flowed over her, until her teacher snapped, "Stupid!" and made her read it over again.

Master Gourami was kind to her. Some of the others were not. The reading teacher was a small, shaggy, sharp-eared creature with slitted eyes that hissed and cursed her slowness. Nevertheless, she learned.

It was in Toadling's nature to try to please. She learned about clothing and bedding and words written down because the goddess had told her to, because her teachers felt it was important. She learned to speak in polite words instead of squalls and to eat dead food without snatching. She memorized things about the human world that she would need to know—that a king was the ruler and a lord was under him and the lord's servants under that.

(Her understanding was spotty at best. Toadling thought for a long time that the king must be like the Eldest and pictured a massive, swollen human that gathered the lords up in his arms and held them while they slept. When she tried to explain this to Master Gourami, he put his head down on the table and the hairs in his ears rippled with laughter.)

She learned that her ideas of beauty were wrong and of no use to anyone. In her world, the Eldest was the most beautiful, swollen with power and secrets and the deaths of her enemies. Duckwight was beautiful, with her patience and her quick, many-jointed fingers. Reedbones, who had enormously long, thin arms and who could swim side to side like an eel, swifter than a kelpie could run, was beautiful.

Toadling, who was small and slow and could not breathe water, did not consider herself beautiful, but it hurt to learn that she was homely and her family were considered among the most hideous of Faerie.

She had been there for nearly a month before Master Gourami told her what she was.

He did it almost by accident. He was trying to teach her a small bit of magic, enough to light a candle, and she was failing wretchedly at it.

"This should be easy," he said wearily, rubbing his face. "Even for someone born human."

"What?" she said.

He blinked at her, and she at him, and then he said, half in a whisper, "Did the greenteeth never tell you?"

"Tell me what?"

And he said the word *changeling* to her, and it, too, slipped down into her heart and rang like a bell under her rib cage.

He was kind and he did not mean to be cruel. He had no way to know that the word would pluck her away from the monsters who loved her. On the far side of *changeling,* they did not belong to her, nor she to them.

So he told her about the games fairies play with mortals, and the echoes that rang between the two kingdoms, and how she had been born in that other kingdom, instead of this one. She felt every word taking her a little farther away from the greenteeth and bringing her no closer to the humans she should have been.

And it occurred to her at last to ask the question that she should have asked the hare goddess: "Who is my father?"

Master Gourami ran his hands over his long, restless whiskers. "A human king," he said. "Barely a king at all, in truth. He holds less land than a horse could cross from dawn to noon."

"She said"—Toadling made a gesture toward the window, toward the moon and the sky and the world, and Master Gourami nodded—"that my father's house would have need of me."

"Yes," said her teacher. "I have been watching, and it seems likely."

Toadling wrapped her arms around herself. She felt ill and her skin felt dry. She was always dry in this place. She did not care about her father, or a mortal kingdom. She wanted running water and deep river hollows dappled with leaves.

"It has been five days, in the mortal world, since you were taken." He smiled faintly. "And so I have another few years to teach you what I can, and then I will send you back to the mortal world so that you may arrive on the seventh day, to stand as godmother to the child left in your place."

CHAPTER 4

When Toadling heard the sound of hooves, she closed her eyes briefly and thought, *Not another one!*

She would not approach this one. She would not. She could not be trusted to speak to humans. Halim had gone away, and if the gods looked kindly on one small toad, he would not come back. She did not think she could handle another one.

The hoofbeats separated out into two beasts, one large, one small. Toadling hopped to the edge of the brambles and looked out.

Apparently, the gods had other people to look after. It was Halim, and he had brought another mule with him.

I won't go out. He'll leave soon enough if he doesn't see me.

"Mistress Toadling!" called the knight. "Mistress Toadling, it's me! Halim! Will you speak to me again?"

"Go away!" said Toadling, standing up and breaking her promise to herself immediately.

He turned toward the sound of her voice. By the fine bones of its face, the mule was none too young, and weighted down with packs.

"I brought things to break curses," he said. "I didn't know who cursed you, or how, so I brought as many as I could find." He gestured toward the mule. "There's moly and salt and rowan and rue and candles, and a knife that my mother's imam said duas over and also I had it blessed by the Benedictine monk who ran the library, so between the two of them, it ought to be quite holy by now. I couldn't find a rabbi. Well, I did, but he wanted to come along because he'd never met a fairy, and I thought you wouldn't like that."

Toadling began to laugh because if she didn't, she would cry immediately. "I told you, I wasn't cursed!"

Cursed by fortune. Cursed by circumstance. Cursed to be whatever I am . . .

Halim seemed unbothered by this. "We'll work something out."

He led the mule and his horse to the place he had camped before and built up a fire. Toadling followed, feeling giddy and despairing and mad. "Please . . ." she said, and could not think how to end the sentence, even when he looked up at her and waited.

"It will be all right," he said, after it became obvious she wasn't going to speak. "If I can make it right, I will."

She should have told him to leave. She knew it.

She sat down at the fire with him and ate bread with salt on it. She had not tasted bread in two hundred years. The taste of the salt was so sharp on her tongue that she thought she might cry again.

"Is that the curse breaking?" asked Halim, watching her closely.

"It's been a long time since I had salt," she said. "The larder lasted me a long time, but eventually it ran out . . . I should not tell you this."

Why not? He knows there's a keep. He knows there's a spell. What am I trying to hide?

He smiled and passed her more salt. She did not think that he could afford it. Salt was very dear and he was a poor knight, but he gave it to her without grudging, and she took it gratefully.

"Tomorrow," said Halim. "Tomorrow we will try to break the curse."

"And if, as I keep saying, there is no curse?"

"Then I will brave the keep for you, Mistress Toadling. I have brought climbing equipment and an axe. The monk said that there aren't that many curses that can hold up to an axe."

"He sounds very wise, this monk," said Toadling. "I wish he'd been wise enough to tell you to stay away."

"He is as curious as I am. It's a dangerous thing, curiosity." He smiled ruefully. "I always thought that I was doing well. So few knights own anything more than their horse and their armor, so they go and fight in tourneys for purses or go off to be mercenaries for coin, and then half the time they gamble it all away after. And I hate gambling, and I don't really want to beat other men bloody for a purse, particularly not when they're friends of mine. But it turns out that if you dangle a mystery in front of me . . . Well, here I am." He made the little head dip that served him for a bow.

"But you *are* like any other knight," she said bitterly. "You want to rescue the beautiful maiden in the tower."

"Well, if she's there, I suppose it's only polite to rescue her. Though I'm embarrassed to say that some of my fellow knights would probably only be interested if the maiden had a treasure to go along with her."

"There's no treasure."

"I didn't think there was. I mostly came for answers. Or maybe just the story."

Toadling sighed. She did not know how to fight a story.

She had learned so many from the greenteeth and later from Master Gourami, but no one had taught her how to stop one.

It occurred to her that she should probably kill Halim in his sleep.

The thought came and squatted on her heart, and she squirmed away from it. There had been so much killing. The queen and the nursemaid . . . though not the dog, they had gotten the dog away in time. Perhaps others that they had never found. It seemed likely.

And they would all be dead of old age now anyway. Does it matter?

Halim smiled at her over the fire, and she took another bite of bread and tasted salt like blood across it.

The christening was not lavish. There were no silk ribbons on the baby's basket, no well-wishing throng. There was a priest, and the lord who was only barely a king, and the mother and a handful of servants.

And Toadling.

She walked into the little chapel expecting to be challenged at every turn, but she was not.

Her courage had failed her completely, but her training had not. Master Gourami had drilled her on this. She had practiced a hundred times or a thousand. In the last year of her training, he had taken her to a dozen different fairy courts, and at every one, over and over, he had found a door and a room and drilled her on the christening.

It was a strange thing, perhaps, to have practiced. It was not like magic or courtesy or the letters that still lay uneasily on her tongue. It would be over in a few minutes, and then what good would that year of her life have been?

But Master Gourami knew what manner of clay he had to shape, and when Toadling stood on the steps and looked up at the open doorway, she did not begrudge a single hour of that year.

Go up the steps. These are like the steps in the houses of the Adhene, rough-cut stone worn down by feet. I have gone up steps like these before.

The doorway was open, and there was a guard on it. He was not a man-at-arms, though, expecting warfare, but a man barely older than a boy. He gaped at her, presumably because he had just seen her spring up from the ground, a woman clad in cracked clay and toad skin.

In the last year of her training, she had been challenged by everything from armed men to magisters, priests who flung holy water in her face, hostile fae, and even once a nun. (The nun was a real human who lived in Faerie. She had come long ago and stayed, and time had run the wrong direction for her. "There is no sense in going back," she said. "I will fall to dust in a heartbeat, like the Children of Lir. And it is only meet that the Church have a representative here in this unshriven land." She was a close friend of Master Gourami's, and Toadling had admired her and feared her in equal measure.)

The hostile fae had been the only ones who could stop her, in practice, and Master Gourami had eventually moved on. "I doubt they will send anyone to protect a changeling," he said. "And if they do . . . well. I suppose we will simply deal with it somehow."

Since Toadling had no idea what that somehow would entail, she was glad to see that it was only a young man.

Go past the guard. Enchant him if you can. Kill him if you must.

She held up a hand and said, "Peace," to him. "I mean no harm."

His mouth moved, but no sound came out. She laid a little charm on him, only a little one: *all is well; this is not your problem.*

His face relaxed. His chin sagged to his chest, as if he might fall asleep. Toadling looked past him to the chapel door.

In their practice, sometimes it was open. Sometimes it was closed. Sometimes there were locks and bars and iron gratings. Sometimes people poured boiling water down on her from the murder holes above, but water had always been her friend. It had coursed over her, deliciously wet, the steam hissing delight against her skin, and then puddled at her feet, and Master Gourami had said, "*Well,*" several times, while his long whiskers twitched in surprise.

There were no locks or bars or boiling water. Toadling stepped through the door, into the chapel, where the parents who did not know her were standing over the child who had taken her place.

In the morning, as good as his word, Halim brought out his implements for breaking curses.

"Tell me at once if this hurts," he said anxiously.

Toadling shook her head, bemused at him for his eagerness and at herself for not running away. "All right," she said. "If this will make you happy."

It could not be said that it went well, but neither did it go badly. She sat patiently while he sprinkled holy water on her, and lit candles in a circle, and recited verses from the Quran, none of which did anything.

"Oh dear," said Halim. "I suppose I should try the Christian prayer to be thorough, but I suspect that my mother wouldn't appreciate it. And I don't know if that's blasphemy or not, and it's probably bad form to blaspheme while you're breaking a curse."

"I'll do it," said Toadling, and launched into the Lord's Prayer. "Our Father, who art in heaven . . ."

The words twisted around in her throat, as her fairy gift tried to recast them in the modern tongue. She had learned the prayer two hundred years ago to please the priest, and the words on her heart were different than the ones on her tongue.

Halim waited politely, but nothing happened.

"Next?" said Toadling.

"I'm supposed to hurl this mixture of moly and salt in your face," he said doubtfully. "But that seems quite hostile."

"Do it." She closed her eyes. She felt an absurd smile on her face and couldn't quite stop it.

He still could not bring himself to hurl the mixture. She felt salt and herbs patter gently on her cheek. It did exactly nothing.

"Last one," said Halim. "Um. I'm supposed to nick you with the blessed knife."

She held out her hand.

He looked from the knife to her, back to the knife. She was surprised to see he'd gone a little green.

"Aren't you a knight?" she asked. "Haven't you stabbed people before?"

"Very few," he said. "And they were all trying to stab me first."

She laughed and took the knife from him.

It was not hard. Master Gourami's spells had often involved a drop of blood to bind them. She prodded the ball of her thumb with the tip and felt the skin part.

Cold steel was never kind to fairies, but those born human were safe enough. Her blood was darker and thinner than Halim's would be, and she suspected that the cut would itch for a few days, but that was all.

She flipped the knife around and offered him the hilt.

"Is the curse broken?" he asked.

"There really isn't one," she said. "Not on me."

He sighed. "I suppose I'll have to climb the tower, then."

She winced and her smile faded.

How can a man who couldn't bear to even nick me possibly stand up to her? He'll get in and see her, and then he'll think I've been lying and wake her and . . .

"I wish you wouldn't," she said.

"It seems like it's the only way to set you free."

Toadling shook her head. "I don't know why you're doing this!"

"Well." Halim busied himself putting away the salt and the herbs. "There's the mystery, of course. But also . . ."

"Also?"

"I would like to save you." He looked slightly embarrassed by the admission. "I have never been of much use to anyone, you see."

"I'm not exactly a fair maiden to be saved by a questing knight," she said. "It's not as if I'm beautiful."

"No," said Halim. "I know I should say that you are, because that would be chivalrous. But I'm not handsome, either, and I'm not rich, and men don't feel the slightest urge to follow me into battle, and I already told you about the tourneys, so I've failed on most counts as a knight. It would be nice to do something and not fail at it. And you're . . . um." He shrugged. "Interesting. And sad."

Toadling had been sad for a long time, but she was not used to being interesting. She had been nearly invisible for so long in her father's house that it surprised her.

"Interesting," she said. "Huh."

"And you look a bit like my friend Faizan used to, when he'd done something wrong and was waiting for his mother to find out," said Halim. "His mother was much fiercer than mine. But he always said the dread was the worst."

The words slid under her ribs like the blessed knife had not. Toadling's breath came out in a short, pained huff.

He was not wrong. She had lived in dread for two hundred years.

He was going to climb the tower, and she could think of no way to stop him.

And inside, some tiny mad voice was saying, *Perhaps it will be all right.*

"Tomorrow," she said shortly. "Bring the knife."

G o through the chapel door," Master Gourami said, "and find the cradle. You must lay this gift on her, that she does no harm." He sat back in the chair, with the firelight lying over his face, casting shadows in violet and gold.

Toadling sat as far from the fire as she could, with her feet in a basin of water. It helped her think, and when she could no longer bear to think, it soothed her a little.

"Will they try to stop me?" she asked.

"A godmother's gift cannot be ungiven. And we will practice," said Gourami firmly. "I will not send you unprepared."

And he had not. Toadling could not fault him.

The fault was mostly her own.

When she stepped through the chapel door, there had been a man standing there, and she thought, *Is that my father?*

He wore robes and a cross around his neck. He stood behind the basket—not a cradle at all, just a little woven thing with an infant in it—and his mouth hung open in surprise as he looked at her.

Toadling knew that she might have to fight her father, though she was under orders not to kill him—it was important that she not kill him, something the fairies wanted done, or not done—and so Master Gourami had given her a dozen charms to stop a man in his tracks, and one powerful one of healing, in case the fight went ill.

This man did not look as if he would try to fight her. He looked old, and the skin around his throat was loose and thick.

"What is this?" cried another man, rising up from the floor. He had been kneeling. He was younger and not terribly large, but his clothes were so layered in so many heavy fabrics and furs that it made him look like a barrel. "Who—"

And then he looked full in Toadling's face, and his voice stuttered to a halt.

Toadling thought, *Of course, I am a fool—this is my father. The old man is the priest.*

Her father, the king.

The king's lips twisted back, and she watched emotions slide across his face—shock, disgust, and finally fear. She wondered if she should be feeling something. *This is my father. This man is my father.*

But Master Gourami had trained her well. The words landed inside her head as if muffled by leaves. The deep pool of her soul did not ripple. She waited for him to attack, with a charm on her tongue.

Fear, it turned out, made him courteous. "I beg your pardon, Fair One," he said, and put a hand across his chest. "We did not expect to be . . . honored."

This, too, she had practiced. Toadling tilted her head an inch, for fairies do not bow to kings, and said, "I have come with a gift."

This is your gift, that you will do no harm to those around you.

The words pressed against the back of her teeth, but she did not say them yet.

She wondered, a moment later, how this man managed to be king at all. The lords of Faerie kept their emotions sealed behind walls of ironic laughter, and you did not know if one was going to kill you until after you were dead. This little king heard *gift* and his face showed greed as naked as an unsheathed sword.

". . . no," said a voice as soft and insubstantial as a cobweb, and the king and Toadling turned.

Her first thought was that a hostile fae had come after all. The woman who faced her had skin so pallid that it was nearly translucent, and she swayed like a willow. The tips of her fingers were nearly blue.

A wailing woman, thought Toadling, *a creature of omens and portents—she'll scream in a moment and the walls will fall—*

The woman lunged.

Toadling stepped back with a charm of defense rising to her lips.

She need not have bothered. The woman was not attacking but going for the basket.

She staggered and half fell across it. Another woman

darted forward, catching at her elbow. "My lady, stop! You're not to move like that—"

"No," breathed the pale woman in her cobweb voice. "No, no, leave her alone. Don't curse her, please . . ."

Master Gourami had drilled her on people pleading. Toadling looked down at the pale woman and said automatically, "I mean no harm."

"Get back," said the king, sounding angry. "The Fair One said a gift, not a curse."

"You know what their gifts are like," said the woman, trying to lift the baby's basket with failing arms. She slumped and the maid tried to hold her up, and the king moved awkwardly, wanting to go forward, but that would take him past Toadling, and would that be considered hostile or disrespectful? Would the fairy take back her offer of a gift?

She read all this on his face, and it was only then, belatedly, that the truth came to Toadling.

They had not drilled on this. The woman was five days from the edge of death, and she should not have been out of her bed at all. Master Gourami had not even considered the possibility that she would come to the christening.

Had not considered the possibility that she *could* come.

Toadling stared down at the woman at her feet.

Her lips moved, but she could not say the word aloud. It had no meaning, but it echoed under her ribs until her entire body shook with it.

Mother?

She knew that she should be feeling something. Her mother was lying across her feet, still reaching for the basket, and there was blood slicking the front of her dress.

Her mother had torn something inside, and her movement had opened it up again, and now she was bleeding to death at Toadling's feet.

Toadling stared down at her and her mind was full of waterweed and the Eldest holding out a gray stone with a hole in it, and Duckwight's webbed hand wrapped around hers. Those had been her mothers. What was this woman to her? What should she feel? Something? Nothing?

She crouched down and took her mother's hand.

"Don't curse her," whispered the mortal woman. "Please?"

"I won't," said Toadling. "It's not a curse. It's a gift. I've come to stop her doing harm—"

And the magic struck.

They had never practiced laying the spell on the changeling. That part could not be practiced. It was a spell and she had been given the words and she had recited them so many times that she could say them in her sleep.

This is your gift, that you will do no harm to those around you.

"You must say them correctly," said Master Gourami. "The magic is bound up in the words. If you say them wrong, you could change the spell, and there will be no second chances."

you will do no harm to those around you
you will do no harm to those around you

She had not gotten the words wrong since the first week of practice.

And now, in her muddled explanation to the woman who should have been her mother, she had said too much of the words and she had said them in the wrong order, and now the spell was rising out of her body like a serpent made of steam, writhing into its new shape, and wrapping around the basket with the changeling in it.

"No . . ." whispered Toadling in horror. "No, no, I didn't—I wasn't done—I didn't mean—"

The magic sank into the basket. In it, the child moved and opened its eyes. They were as green as poison and they looked into Toadling's, and the spirit behind them was old and cold and cruel.

And it was done.

The gift was given.

I've come to stop her doing harm.

Her mother lay dying on the stones, and Toadling felt the door to Faerie slam closed behind her.

CHAPTER 5

Toadling had resigned herself to Halim breaching the castle, to . . . whatever came next. But she had forgotten how thick the brambles were, how densely the trees had grown up around the entrances.

"This would be easier if you could turn into a toad," said Toadling, after Halim had been hacking away with a hatchet for several hours.

He raised an eyebrow at her. "I can safely say that in all my life, no one has ever said that to me before," he said. "Can you show me how?"

Toadling considered this briefly. Duckwight had shown her . . . Was it the same?

She took his hand cautiously. His skin felt very warm. She laid her wrist against his and thought about magic running like water over a dam.

A moment later, Halim shouted and tried to catch her as she turned into a toad in midair and tumbled to the ground. "Ack! Mistress Toadling—careful—no—are you *hurt*?"

She got to her feet, laughing. The fall had been negligible, into soft litter, and she had been human again almost as soon as she hit the ground. "I am fine," she said. "But no, I do not think I can teach you. I think . . ." She tried to remember what she knew of magic. Master Gourami had done his best, but greenteeth magic was all instinct and moving water and the magic bound with words had never come easily to her. "I think . . . you are too human." She spread her hands helplessly.

"And you are not," said Halim. Not with censure. Merely a statement.

"Not entirely," she said. "Not anymore." There did not seem to be any point in lying. "I was born human," she said, "but things happened."

"I did not expect all this," he said, "when I went digging through books about a lost keep."

"No," she said with a sigh. "I suppose you didn't."

Halim went back to hacking away at the brambles, and Toadling went back to watching him.

The goddess came to her in the form of a hare two days after the christening, while Toadling crouched, toad shape, in a corner of the stableyard.

"I failed," said Toadling. Toads don't talk as mortals do, but she knew the goddess would understand her croaking.

"Did you?" The hare sat beside the toad, and a little silvery light came down from the moon and lay gently on the warts and hollows of Toadling's back.

"The spell went wrong," said Toadling miserably. "I said the wrong words. I was trying to explain, but I said too many, and I was panicking and it all went wrong together."

"Tell me exactly what you said," said the goddess, and Toadling did.

There was a long silence.

"Where is the mother now?" asked the hare finally, and Toadling felt a strange relief. If the goddess had said *your mother,* it would have been too much to bear. She did not want ownership of these people, or to be owned by them in turn. *Your father's house* was hard enough.

The mother was a creature of the mortal world, and Toadling knew that she was not.

"I healed her," said Toadling. "It was the spell Master Gourami gave me, the one in case I had to fight." She gave a short, harsh laugh, a toad croaking in the gloom. "And it bought me a place here—can you imagine? They think I traded my magic powers to save her life. The king said I would be an honored member of the household. I didn't know how to explain."

"Then don't." The goddess stretched and her ears rippled against her back. "You gave the changeling child a gift, and you cannot take it back."

Toadling blinked at her.

"It's a gift. I've come to stop her doing harm," said the hare. *"That* is what you gave her, for good or ill." She scratched her ears with one back foot, rapid-fire, while Toadling goggled. "It is not what we had hoped for, but it is still a given gift. Now it falls to you to stop her doing harm."

"But how?" whispered Toadling. "How can I do that? How can I stay here?"

The goddess was turning silver now, and Toadling could see the mud of the stable yard through her.

"Learn what you can. Use what you learn. You have not failed yet." She touched her nose briefly to Toadling's and then ran into the moonlight and disappeared.

The changeling child was named Fayette, which was an irony that Toadling's language gift allowed her to appreciate far too well. *Little fairy. Yes, of course.*

She was an odd infant and she grew into an odd toddler, and it became obvious soon enough that there was something that was not-quite-right about her.

"Devil-touched," muttered the wet nurse, crossing herself. But Fayette had been christened and so God presumably knew she existed, and a fairy had given her gifts—and not even the most superstitious of nurses could find it in their heart to be suspicious of Toadling.

Another fairy might have played up their status as exiled healer, demanded special treatment and catering to their every whim. But Toadling tried to be helpful and stammered when she was nervous and had beautiful, worried eyes in a homely face. Her transformation into a toad was shocking, true, but it did not involve any inside-out bits or explosions, and she was such a small, inoffensive toad and such a small, inoffensive human, and she went out of her way to change behind buildings and things where people would not see it and be troubled by it.

When the midwife asked her, very cautiously, what little magics might help in the stillroom, she was so glad to be doing something useful that she came in with armloads of waterweed and rowan and showed the midwife how to tie them up in bundles of red thread, and the maids were three days hanging them in every window of the castle.

"And I thought I'd go blind from all that knotting," said the midwife later, "but she never stopped. Poor thing. I don't think our fairy quite knows what to do with herself."

Toadling, who had excellent hearing, caught this, and *our fairy* warmed her and frightened her in equal measure.

My mother. My father's house. Our fairy. It seemed that this mortal world was determined to lay claim to her in some fashion, whether she wanted it or not.

The years of Fayette's infancy passed with Toadling lurking in corners of rooms, in the cool damp of the cellar, in the muddy corner of the stableyard. She went fishing and brought back her catches, and at first the cook thanked her and threw the fish to the dogs, for fear of magic, and then the cook thanked her and cooked the fish, and eventually the cook no longer thanked her and would say, as she passed, "Fetch some fish if you've a mind, Toadling."

If she had pretended to be a grand person, she might have earned resentment, but as it was, she reaped good-natured contempt. Her status was roughly equal to that of the priest, and he was old and a trifle fuzzy and was also held in affectionate contempt. But he was "our priest" and she was "our fairy," and they were both expected to intercede with other worlds because that was their job.

She wondered sometimes if he felt as frightened and overwhelmed as she did, but unlike most of the castle folk, the priest never forgot that she was an otherworldly being, and he was always stiff and formal and afraid. He taught her the Lord's Prayer, that she might say it and prove herself not a demon thereby, and then he tried to have no more to do with her.

Fayette was weaned early, because the wet nurse said that she was done being bitten and if the king wanted his child nursed, he could do it himself. The king was weak, but he had a sense of humor to make up for it and found this amusing, even if the queen did not.

In the third year, Fayette's tantrums became more and more dangerous. She bit her new nurse's hand down to the bone and tore her mother's hair out of her scalp. If she was slapped, she would launch herself at the attacker with nails and teeth, and since she also did this to anyone who attempted to trim said nails, she left long, jagged scars.

Toadling heard this from her usual place in the court-yard, where she sat toad-belly deep in mud, quiet and out of the way, and knew that it was time.

She did not want to move. She wanted very much to lie in the mud, which lay cool and squelching up around her legs. It held up her weight and curved to her body. She would have liked to never move again.

But she had been given no choice. She had come to stop Fayette from doing harm.

She got to her feet and put on human flesh and went into the nursery.

The nurse saw her first. "A moment only, Mistress Fairy," she begged. "Just . . . just watch her for a moment. Please."

"Yes," said Toadling. "It is why I am here."

The new nurse fled down the steps so fast that Toadling feared for her safety.

In the shadows of the nursery, the changeling moved.

"Listen," Toadling said to Fayette. The girl watched her with fierce, clear eyes, not murky like the waters that Toadling loved. "You don't know what you are yet, but I do. I know. I'll try to help you. But you have to be good. You can do too much harm. You have to try to be good."

Stubborn chin. Savage green eyes. Fayette opened her mouth and Toadling saw the flash of teeth behind her lips.

"No," said Fayette, in her high toddler's voice. "I don't."

It took far longer than Toadling expected for Halim to breach the keep. She had gotten used to the idea that her wards were fragile, and so their strength astonished her now. Days went by with the sound of bark chips flying and Halim's curses—followed immediately by apologies, no matter how often she told him that she was not offended.

"I am sorry," he said. "It is chivalry—no, that isn't true. Actually, it's my mother. If I swore before a lady, she would scold me, so now I apologize instinctively. The apology is part of the curse. If I stub my toe, I say *damnationsorry!*"

Toadling uttered a mild oath in the tongue of greenteeth, which sounded like a bubbling shriek. Halim's eyes went wide.

"Sorry," she said—and then smiled, because now the apology was part of her curse as well. "In the language of the ones who raised me, that is . . . more or less what you said."

"What manner of creatures raised you, if I may ask?"

Toadling was silent for so long that he began to hack at the thorn hedge again. He had reached the dry wood of the heart instead of the living outskirts—thorns die from the inside out, like priests—so the stems no longer bent away from his axe, but the wood was hard as stone and grabbed at the blade when he struck.

"There is no word in your language," she said finally. "I cannot find one in my head. They are water spirits. Like your *marid,* maybe, but small. They live in streams and muddy bogs, not oceans."

"Lesser spirits." Halim nodded. "They say the types of djinn are as many as there are elements of the world." He smiled abruptly. "Of course, the people who say that have likely never met even one. I should be asking you questions about the other world so that I might write a book that tells all the truth, instead."

Toadling swallowed several times. Her mouth felt dry.

"If we live through this," she said quietly, "I will tell you everything I can think of."

He turned so quickly that he nearly dropped the axe and missed slicing his leg open by a handsbreadth. "You'll come with me, then?"

"If you still want me to," she said. "If you do not regret it. Your mother sounds . . . kind." She swallowed again, wondering if kindness would be enough for a toad-girl.

"If we live," he said. A shadow dropped over his eyes. "What is inside the tower is very dangerous, then."

"More than you can imagine."

W hen the queen summoned her, Toadling was startled, then afraid.

They had spoken less than a handful of times. You could not avoid another person in a keep as small as this one, but nevertheless, they had managed. Toadling stayed in her small, inoffensive toad shape when the queen was about and did not ask—or demand—a place in her counsels. The queen did not seek her out. When Toadling watched Fayette, it was with the nurse beside her, not the queen.

But when Fayette was six, the queen summoned the castle fairy to the solar, and Toadling, ever obedient, went.

The solar was empty except for the queen. She was looking out the window, with the sun glowing on her skin.

Toadling knew that to mortal eyes, the queen was beautiful. To Toadling, she seemed pallid and flat-faced, her golden hair lying dead and motionless on her shoulders.

Among the greenteeth, only Fadeweed was that pale. She lurked in the deepest water, where she would not burn, and her paleness was a lure to fish. She would use her fingers as bait, wiggling them like white worms, and then snatch the fish up and bite them behind the eye.

Fadeweed spoke very little, but she shared her fish gener-ously, as if food had taken the place of her words.

The memory rose up like water before her, and so Toad-ling missed the first words that the queen had spoken to her in more than a year.

She bit her lip, hoping that it had not been something that required acknowledgment.

The next words drove it out of her head.

"Fayette tortured a dog this morning," said the queen.

Toadling cringed. "Is . . . is the dog hurt badly?"

The queen turned her head and looked at Toadling for a long, silent time and then said, "It will heal. One of the foresters took it to live outside the keep."

Toadling nodded, weak-bellied with relief.

I've come to keep you from doing harm . . . and again and again, I've failed.

"I'm sorry," she said. "Usually I can catch her before . . ."

The queen looked away, out the window again.

"There have been others, then."

"Yes," said Toadling. She swallowed. "The birds that get into the tower sometimes. And the dovecote. And I think mice, too, but she's gotten better at hiding them after."

"You've punished her for it," said the queen, a line form-ing between her eyebrows.

Toadling wanted to laugh, not from humor but simple frustration. "It doesn't do any good. She's like a cat play-ing. They're not real to her; they're just . . . things that move and flutter and squeak. The nurse has tried—it's not her fault, I swear! But we can't make her believe it matters. I'm sorry."

The queen was silent for a long time.

"You saved my life," she said, and Toadling almost said,

I'm sorry, again but caught herself in time. She was not supposed to apologize for that.

"I wanted to think it was your influence," said the queen. "I wanted to think that you were a wicked fairy who had come to lead my daughter astray. Perhaps saving my life was merely to cover your intentions."

Her voice was toneless, without emotion. Toadling pictured flat water without a ripple, while something roiled in the depths beneath.

"They say that you ask for almost nothing," said the queen. "You eat only fish and you do not fear the touch of holy water or iron. You help in any small way you can." She turned at last and looked Toadling full in the face. "And the toad is one of the devil's animals, they say, but I think he would come in a pleasing guise, not . . ." She flicked her fingers, taking in Toadling's ugliness and then dismissing it.

Toadling said nothing. She thought perhaps that she should feel something, knowing that her mother found her ugly, but she did not. *I am probably doing this wrong again,* she thought, *not feeling something when I should.*

She looked down at her hands, at the scar where the Eldest had marked her. *No. I have many mothers. If I am hideous, then we are hideous together.* And that made it easier, because in her heart of hearts, she could not believe that her mothers were anything but beautiful.

"I wanted to believe that you were the cause," said the queen. "Because there is something very wrong with my daughter. But the nurse says that when she is at her worst, you will leap in. She scratches and claws you as much as the rest of us, and she does not obey you any more than she obeys me. And you endure this all, without complaint, day after day."

Toadling looked up. "I do complain," she croaked. "At least a little."

The queen's lips curved into the ghost of a smile, but it was fleeting. "I had hoped that you had cursed her," she said. "That your gift was truly a curse. But you didn't, did you?"

Toadling shook her head. "No. She . . . she isn't . . ." No, she could not say that Fayette was a changeling—who would believe her? Someone would ask where the real child was, and what a terrible road *that* would be to walk down.

But the word *curse* inspired her and turned into a half-truth that lay easier on the tongue. "She was cursed, but not by me. By a . . . a different fairy. Before she was born. To be cruel. I was sent to try and stop the curse. I was supposed to give her a gift and leave again, but it didn't go right, and so I'm still here. Trying to help." Toadling shook her head. "I'm sorry. I wish they'd had someone better to send."

"The nurse tells me that we should be glad that you're still here," said the queen. She let out a long sigh. "Can Fayette be cured?"

Toadling shook her head. "Only contained," she said. "I'm sorry."

The queen struck her across the face.

"How dare you fairies meddle in humankind?" she asked. Her voice was still toneless and calm. She might as well not have moved.

Toadling licked blood from her lips. Her head rang, but she had taken worse blows from kelpie hooves.

It did not occur to her to be angry, or to strike back.

"It is sport to some of them," said Toadling, honestly enough. "And others hate that and try to stop it when they can."

"Like angels and devils," said the queen.

Toadling gave a small, unhappy croak of laughter. "I think angels would be better at it than I am."

The queen was silent for a long time. Dust motes moved in the sunlight. Faintly, through the window, Toadling could hear the sounds of the chickens clucking and a stable hand singing to himself.

Finally, the queen said, "I do not believe that a devil would have asked about the dog."

Toadling blinked at her.

"Contain her as best you can," said the queen. "And if you find a way to lift this curse, tell me. No matter what it takes."

"I . . . I'll do my best . . ." said Toadling.

The queen nodded and turned back to the window. Toadling took it as dismissal and crept away, down the turning spiral stairs.

Thinking, *The only curse is that she is a changeling. And she will be as cruel as she can, because that is the nature of changelings. Good spirits do not steal away babies to take their place. It is only the wicked that are sent to make mischief.*

And only the dutiful that are sent to try and stop them.

The queen's handprint across her face left a black bruise, the color of Toadling's tears. There was no hiding it and it would not have occurred to Toadling to try to do so, but people noticed.

When they saw the handprint, they saw Toadling behind it, and that she did not like. She had worked too hard to go unnoticed.

She had not thought to dodge. Greenteeth did not slap

one another—not out of any virtue, but because a slap was such a useless thing underwater. When greenteeth brawled, it was with teeth and strangling fingers, spines and claws. Toadling had no claws, but she had learned early how to bite.

Thinking of it now—of the uselessness of human hands—Toadling had to smile. She had been so young when she snapped back at one of the greenteeth who had stolen a bit of her fish. And the Eldest had laughed and laughed at her tiny ferocity, and the thief laughed, too, and surrendered the fish, and Toadling had felt proud and bold and dangerous. She had probably been about four years old.

But her smile faded soon enough. Unlike Toadling, Fayette truly was dangerous, and there was so little that Toadling could do to hold her in check.

Perhaps if there had been another fairy. Even one as weak as Toadling herself. Then it would have been easier—or if it was not easier, at least there would have been someone else to talk to.

There was the nurse, of course. Toadling still had no idea what her name was. She addressed her as "Nurse," and the nurse addressed Toadling as "Mistress," the same as she addressed the midwife and the leech. Nurse and mistress, shoved together by fate, trying to control a creature that only looked like a child.

Toadling took her smallest, sulkiest toad form and lurked in the cellar, in the cool space under the barrels.

If I am wishing for help, I might as well wish for Master Gourami, or the Eldest. Or a great lord of elves, perhaps . . .

A great lord of elves would likely have been a greater horror than a dozen Fayettes. He could have unmade the entire keep, danced the inhabitants to death, turned the queen's eyes into dragonflies, and laughed as they flew away.

Or then again, perhaps he wouldn't. Perhaps the weak king would say something to amuse him, or an interesting cloud would come by and he would be distracted long enough to forget the little castle and the little king entirely.

But it was that kind of twisting, careless mind that Toadling was up against. Fayette was a creature of one of those great lords—cruel and charming and beautiful almost to the point of pain.

I can overpower her now only because I am so much older, thought Toadling, and she gave a hoarse croak at that, because she was not in human shape and could not laugh. *And perhaps, a little, because she has no one to teach her subtlety . . .*

She could almost have felt sorry for Fayette, who was alone in the same way that Toadling was alone . . .

. . . except for the dog.

The dog . . . and the chickens and the lambs and the cat and ask me again next week . . . Toadling grimaced. She had kept Fayette from most of the animals—and indeed, the rooster had been more than capable of defending his ladies without any help from a fairy!—but anything small or easily frightened was easy prey.

She had gone to the priest years ago, when she began to realize that Fayette was beyond her power to contain. "You have to talk to her," she begged him. "You have to explain to her. I'm trying. I can't."

The old priest looked at her with his weak, watery eyes. "She is not of the age of discretion," he said. "Teach her her catechism."

Toadling gripped the sides of her head, trying not to scream. She did not teach Fayette anything. She could sometimes trick her into learning by telling her that she was too young to understand.

"Spare the rod," he said, "and spoil the child."

"Please," said Toadling, with all the patience she possessed. "I beg you. Her soul needs more than rods."

The priest scowled, but he knew his duty. Perhaps it shamed him to be reminded of it by a fairy.

Fayette met with him twice, while he lectured her. The third time, hours passed, and at last Toadling crept into the tiny chapel and found the old priest dead with no mark on him.

"He turned a color," said Fayette, who was playing with bits of the Eucharist on the floor. "And fell over."

"You didn't tell anyone," said Toadling softly, wondering how long the priest had taken to die.

She did not . . . quite . . . think that Fayette had killed him, but she could imagine the girl crouched beside him, watching with interest while he gasped and clawed at the air.

Fayette hunched up one shoulder in a shrug. Obviously, she had not.

They buried the priest in the graveyard. It was not long afterward that Fayette had begun tormenting animals. The nurse and Toadling, after that, took care to never leave her unattended.

And to think that once she had thought that she might be able to teach Fayette to be good!

She began to laugh again, and the sound of croaking echoed from the stones and filled the cellar, although there was no one else to hear.

CHAPTER 6

Is it a lindworm?" asked Halim.

Toadling cocked her head sideways, puzzled.

They were sitting around the fire. Halim had stopped cutting when it grew so dark that he could no longer see the axe. "And chopping my foot off would be a foolish way to end my quest and would do you no good at all. Although it would likely not surprise my mother."

He had eaten and shared his food with Toadling. As a toad, a few snapped-up beetles would suffice, but it had been a long time since she ate human food. She tried not to eat too much, though he shared generously. She wished that she had something to share in return, but it seemed unlikely that he would appreciate beetles.

"A lindworm?" she said. Her word gift gave her too many choices, some of which made no sense at all. "Like . . . a serpent?"

"A dragon," said Halim.

"Oh! Do you still have dragons, then?"

Halim opened his mouth and closed it again. "It occurs to me," he said, after a moment, "that perhaps you should be telling me the answer to this question, not the other way around. Do we?"

"Not that I know," admitted Toadling. "Dragons love fouled, empty places. But they are too large. They cannot keep themselves quiet, so heroes stand against them. Most of them are dead now, or gone away." She tried to remember what Master Gourami had said. The word *dragon* woke too many different chains of thoughts, and then she had to sort through them, the way that the queen had sorted through different colors of thread to make a tapestry, and that image woke another chain of thoughts—*the queen ice pale, the earth falling black against her skin, the black handprint seen in reflected water*—

"Dragons," said Halim gently, when a long time had passed.

"Oh! Yes!" Toadling caught herself. "Yes. They kill them in Faerie, too, if they catch them. Magic doesn't work, you see, only swords." She wound her fingers together. "There is a story that they brought a knight in to kill one once."

"Really? Through a fairy mound or some such?"

"Yes. They led his horse and put a magic on him to fight the dragon." She shook her head. "But they did it wrong. Master Gourami—the one who taught me—he said they were fools. They should have just asked. But they put a charm on him to force him. So he killed the dragon, but he left the eggs, and they hatched out. He must have known they would. When they tried to find him again, to kill the hatchlings, he had gone to the sea."

"Does that work?" asked Halim.

Toadling nodded. "The sea has its own gods," she said.

They sat there for a little time, while the fire popped and crackled. It had never occurred to Toadling to go to sea. A little salt she liked, but the sea would be too much for her. The water was her friend, but the sea was too vast. It would engulf her like a lover, and she would die of salt-poison in its embrace.

"So not a dragon, then," said Halim.

"No," said Toadling. A dragon would be easier in some ways. Halim would never see a dragon and think that it was innocent and beautiful. "Not a dragon."

The nurse died on a clear day in October. Toadling found her at the foot of the tower stairs, with Fayette sitting on the steps with her chin in her hand.

Toadling cursed, a garbled greenteeth curse, and dropped to her knees. There was a great deal of blood, mostly under the nurse's head, and no chance at all that she was alive.

"*What happened?!*" cried Toadling in anguish.

"She fell," said Fayette, looking at the body with interest. There was blood all over her arms, though she seemed unhurt. "Down the stairs, over and over, like the tumblers." (There had been tumblers at a fair some weeks earlier, to Fayette's great fascination.) "I wish she'd do it again. It was funny to watch."

Toadling stared at her in silent horror.

"I tried to pick her up," said Fayette. "To take her to the top and watch it again. But she's too heavy." She screwed up her flexible child's face in a scowl. "And I tried to do it the other way, you know, but it isn't easy . . ."

Toadling's mind was blank and silent.

"Like this," said Fayette, and the nurse's arm began to move.

Her hand rose straight up in the air, dragging the wrist with it. For a horrible moment, Toadling thought that the nurse was still alive despite her injuries, and then she felt the magic.

No. No!

It was a jabbing, prickly magic, all edges. It wrapped in a loop around the dead nurse's arm and pulled upward.

It was coming from Fayette.

Toadling's magic was all mud and water, but she made that into a blanket and threw it over the nurse, smothering the flame of Fayette's power. The nurse's hand flopped back down, lifeless.

"Hey!" said Fayette. She looked from the nurse's hand to Toadling and back again. "You did that!" And then, as astonishment bloomed into outrage, "*You?*"

Her white skin went suddenly red and mottled with fury, for Fayette had not yet learned to be angry beautifully, and she rose to her feet, clenching her fists.

Toadling could not bear it. Not standing over the nurse's body, which had not yet gone cold. She turned blindly and ran from the foot of the tower.

She grabbed the first person she saw—one of the stable boys, come inside on an errand—and clutched his arm. "Help," she said. "Help, please—the herbwife—the priest—the king—someone, please, *help!*"

The stable boy did not listen. He was staring past her, his face slack with horror. Toadling felt her magic tearing, the water boiling away.

She turned.

The nurse staggered out of the tower, head flopping bonelessly on the end of her neck, and Fayette giggled and Toadling gave up and simply screamed.

W hat is to be done?" asked the queen, after the horror had finally ended, after Fayette had been bundled off to her room and Toadling sat in the queen's solar, her skin as gray as the corpse that Fayette had made walk.

No one had doubted Toadling. That was the thing that shocked her the most. No one had doubted. All the years she had spent in the keep, thinking of herself as nothing, assuming that she would go unbelieved . . . and they had believed her when she had said that it was Fayette.

Even humans are capable of seeing evil when it lives among them, she thought, slow and stumbling, as if reading unfamiliar words on a page. *Even they have noticed.*

"I don't know," said Toadling. She covered her face. "I can't watch her every hour. I have to sleep sometimes. I thought she was afraid of the nurse enough . . . or . . . or the nurse was older, and children obey adults, I thought— but now she's learned she doesn't have to . . . I don't *know*!"

"I will not kill my own child," said the king, looking proud and noble and resolute, which lasted until he folded his lips together and said helplessly, "Someone else will have to do it."

"You will not kill Fayette!" snapped the queen. "It isn't her fault! She is my beautiful daughter, and one of *them* has cursed her!" She slapped at the air in Toadling's direction, and then added, "Not you," over her shoulder. Toadling shrugged.

"Making a corpse dance is well beyond curses," said the king dully. "She did that. I saw it. We all saw it. By rights she should be burned at the stake."

The desire to say, *Yes, do that,* reared up so strong in Toadling's breast that it shocked her, and she realized that she hated Fayette, she who had never hated anyone.

You could not hate a child—only a monster would hate a child—but the child was a monster in the shape of a child, an elfin creature whose power was only contained by her youth and her unfamiliarity with the world.

I should kill her, realized Toadling numbly. *I should have killed her years ago. Gourami and the goddess sent the wrong person. They should have sent someone ruthless enough to have strangled her in the crib. Oh goddess! I cannot do this! I have never killed anything fiercer than a fish!*

"Where is she now?" asked the king.

"Sleeping," said Toadling. "The power she used was exhausting. She will sleep for some time."

"If only she could sleep forever," he muttered, and Toadling's head snapped up.

Sleep.

She could not bring herself to kill Fayette, perhaps, but she could put the changeling girl to sleep.

"I . . . I might be able to keep her asleep . . ." she said. "For a little while, at least."

The king and queen looked at each other, then at her. Toadling saw them as they were in that moment, two parents: one weak, one strong in the wrong places; two people who didn't even like each other very much but had been thrust together by the world and viewed one another as necessary evils.

The words *mother* and *father* never crossed her mind.

"Tell us what you need," said the king.

"Water," said Toadling. "A great deal of it. And we'll hope that it's enough."

They filled the courtyard with barrels, with pots, with jars, with anything that would hold an ounce of liquid. The old wheelbarrow with swelled boards was brought in from the garden, filled to the rim. Toadling looked at it and nearly laughed with despair, it was so little.

"Not enough," she said. "This is not enough." She picked up a shovel and felt the earth with her bare toes, walking through the courtyard. "Here. Dig here."

The guards and the serving folk looked at the king, and the king took the shovel in his own hands and began to dig.

They brought shovels and picks and plain wooden boards. They used their hands and dug down into the soft ground to find the hidden water.

Occasionally they looked up toward the tower, where Fayette still was sleeping, and then they would dig faster.

Toadling knew the shape of what she was doing, but she had no idea if it was even possible. All the charms that Master Gourami had given her were used up. She had only her own water magic, her own tiny charms, the ones that Duckwight had woken under her skin.

She could call fish to the surface of the water, though it still took her own two hands to catch them. She could tie hair into elf-knots. And she could still the surface of the water, quiet the ripples disturbing it, turn it into a little flat mirror untroubled by wind or wave.

Fayette was fire and air and fury, and Toadling could not hold her, but she did not need to be held. She needed to be quieted.

She had done it several times before, when someone could not sleep and the herbwife was half-mad with impatience. It took a little water, usually no more than a cup held between her palms, and she stilled the water and quieted the patient, and then, usually, they could sleep. Toadling had quieted the stable master's son during his fever, and the herbwife swore that she had saved him.

"Not that he'd have died," she had muttered, "but I was like to throttle him if he did not stop his whining."

But Fayette was no human child. Toadling might as well have thrown a cup of water onto a bonfire.

She needed more. As much water as the people could bring her, as much as she could call up from the earth itself.

The king was standing calf-deep in water now, and Toadling did not know if it would be enough.

When do I tell them to stop? When do I start the spell? What if I can't do it at all?

She thought she could. She had used it a time or two on Fayette already, to make her sleep a little longer, because it was simply so much easier when Fayette was asleep.

To keep her asleep forever . . . well.

It does not need to be forever. It only needs to be until . . . until I think of something else. Until one of them gets tired of never entering the tower and decides to kill her, or the king finds his courage, or the whole place catches fire and burns down around our ears.

When the king was nearly up to his knees in the water and the stable master had thrown off the lid on the well, Toadling thought, *I am stalling and now I must actually do the spell.*

She knelt down in the pool of water and gestured for the diggers to move back. Her feet sank into the muddy bottom, and she hooked her toes deeply into it. Her skin sang with the water's touch, because skin was foolish and did not always know when it should be afraid.

She began to pull the power up into herself, drinking it in, shoving it into the hollow pockets under her skin until she felt as huge and bloated as the Eldest. She wished desperately that she was that huge, that she had that kind of strength. The Eldest had more power in one webbed hand than Toadling had in her entire body. An untrained change-ling would have presented her with no more challenge than a duckling. She could have put the girl to sleep for a thousand years, or turned her into a fish, or . . .

The Eldest could have wrung Fayette's neck without a second thought, she thought bleakly, and hated herself for envying that.

Ultimately, though, the spell was not difficult. It was a blanket laid over the sleeper, a single command: *Sleep. Sleep and do not wake.*

Fayette was exhausted from making the dead walk and did not fight.

Sleep. Sleep forever. Sleep until the world ends.

She poured the power out from beneath her skin, filling the stone tower with sleep. It exhausted her, and yet Toadling felt as if the spell was so simple, so obvious that she should be ashamed of herself. *Someone else would do it better. Someone else would be more clever.*

No one else was here.

She opened her eyes and found that it was nearly dark, and the mud had dried around her feet.

"Is it done?" whispered the king, when she stepped out of the mud and it cracked and crackled around her toes.

Toadling nodded.

"Now what?" asked the queen.

"Now we go and see if it worked," croaked Toadling.

S tepping into the tower felt like stepping into a lake. Condensation ran down the inside of the stones, and the air was so humid it was almost fog. The magic pulsed and pounded like blood. Toadling looked at the king and queen behind her, and they did not seem to notice.

In the tower room, Fayette slept.

She lay curled on her side, a faint smile on her lips. She looked angelic, but Toadling had had long years to become used to that. She looked at the beautiful golden-haired child and felt only guilt and grief and weariness.

The queen reached down to stroke the hair out of Fayette's face, and Toadling moved faster than she ever had in her life, seizing the queen's wrist before her fingers could touch the changeling's skin.

"Don't touch her," she said. "I can't keep her asleep if you touch her. I know I can't."

The queen inhaled sharply and withdrew her hands. She folded them together under her breasts and stared down at Fayette, who was frowning now and mumbling in her sleep.

"She senses that you're here, I think," said Toadling.

"I thought . . ." The queen, for once, looked uncertain. "I thought perhaps my presence . . . I thought it might give her a little peace . . ."

You fool, thought Toadling wearily. *You poor fool. You have poured out love, and backed it with all the steel you possess, on a creature that does not love you and never will. And I am more a fool because I did not know how to stop you.*

"I do not know if there is much peace in her, Your Highness," she said.

"What do we do now?" asked the king.

"You can kill her," said Toadling wearily, "if you are very quick. Or you can lock her up here in the tower and never touch her."

"Will it hurt her? Won't she starve?" asked the queen.

She's a changeling. She'll live halfway to forever in a magic sleep. She wouldn't even notice. I don't know if she'll even bother to age.

Aloud she said only, "She will take no harm of it. You have my word."

"Then we will lock her up," said the queen, and the king bowed his head, acquiescing to her will.

They closed the nursery door and barred it, then bricked up the tower door for good measure. The mason looked to Toadling for final approval, and Toadling hardly knew what to say.

"You know brick and stone," she said to him. "I only know mud and water. What does the brick tell you?"

"It tells me that it will do its best," said the mason, and then put a hand over his mouth, as if his own words had shocked him.

"Good," said Toadling. "Good. That's all that we can do."

Halim reached the keep walls the next day.

He stared at the stone for a long time, holding the axe in one hand and scratching the back of his neck with the other. He seemed baffled as if, having looked for the keep, he had not actually expected to find it.

"What now?" he said, almost to himself. "I cannot cut through stone . . ."

"There's an entrance," said Toadling. "To the left, about five yards."

"Should I cut to it?" he asked. "Or simply climb over?"

Toadling shrugged.

"Is the inside . . . ?"

"Clearer," she said. "There are some trees, but it does not grow in the same way."

He nodded, turned to the left, and began to chop and pry his way along the wall.

His work went more swiftly now, as he only had to force the stems away from the wall. He left a cramped tunnel behind him, studded with jagged stems. Toadling dropped into toad shape and hopped along beside him, in the shadow of the broken branches.

"I have a horror that I will fall," he told her conversationally, using the axe handle to lever a twisted trunk aside. "And one of these stubs that I've left will catch me in the thigh, right where the big artery is, and I will bleed out before I can finish cursing. And even then I will probably apologize for having cursed. My last words will be *I'm sorry.*"

Toadling croaked a laugh. It was funny and it hurt, because she was nearly certain that her last words would also be *I'm sorry,* or perhaps just stammering as she tried to get an apology out.

"Ah, you are a toad again." He swung the axe, then grunted as the blade bound into the dead wood and he had to wiggle it loose. "It's for the best, I suppose. Toads probably don't trip and fall and impale themselves on broken branches. I am feeling guilty enough for having bothered you. If you tripped on a branch, I would likely expire from guilt. The Brother Librarian said that I was almost guilt-ridden enough to join a monastery, but our faith does not have an equivalent. And if I expired from guilt, my mother would be very upset, and I would have to feel guilty about that, too. I'm babbling now, aren't I?"

"Somewhat," said Toadling, turning back into a human in a little space in the thorns.

"I thought so. I do that when I don't know what to say. I talk to fill spaces. I'm a wretched liar. Although a good liar would probably say that, wouldn't they?"

Toadling shrugged. Lies had never been any great part of her life, except for the one about Fayette's curse. The truth had been more than difficult enough.

The greenteeth had never told her that she was human, but it did not have the feel of a lie. She had never asked. The greenteeth had not told her. They had not cared. It was of no more import than Fadeweed's paleness or Reedbones's speed. She was theirs; they were hers. The love of monsters was uncomplicated.

Halim reached the entryway to the keep and grunted in surprise. It was much clearer inside, with a few large trees and rank growth of weeds, but without the smothering brambles.

He looked up at the sky, a broad square visible above the walls. "Not that late. Hmm . . ."

"Not tonight," said Toadling. "Please."

He looked over at her, surprised. "No? You don't want to . . . to get this over with?" He gestured vaguely toward the ruined building with his axe.

She shook her head. "We'll have a fire," she said. "And I'll tell you . . . well. I'll tell you the rest of it."

"All right," he said. "If you're sure."

Toadling nodded.

CHAPTER 7

The keep lasted perhaps five years after that. People left and simply did not return. They would go down to the market, out into the woods to hunt, away to drive the sheep to another pasture, and just . . . not come back.

Toadling, squatting in her quietest toad shape beside the tower door, watched the seasons pass and the population of the castle grow smaller and smaller. It was as if the keep had taken an invisible but mortal wound. Its people bled away, drop by drop, and no one tried to staunch the flow.

Did I do this? she wondered. The magic that kept Fayette quiet was a thick blanket inside the tower, but it would be foolish to think that it ended at the tower's walls. The currents and eddies carried throughout the keep, drank endlessly from the well. The speed with which the water dropped had frightened Toadling at first, but then it slowed and the deep spring showed no sign of going dry.

Eventually she realized that the water was being pulled from a vast circle all around the keep, that the fields dried out much more swiftly than they had, that all the neighboring wells were running dry. Guilt gnawed at her for the trees that died, but for the humans who moved away, she felt only relief.

You must get away from here, she told them silently. *You must leave before the magic fails. When Fayette wakes, she will be a horror such as your land has never seen, and I do not think I can stop her twice.*

She still could not believe that she had spun such a large magic.

It became second nature to her within a season, like her own breathing. She had only to let it flow through her, water to power, power to spell. But at the same time, she did not try to change it or adjust it. If the quietness was hard on the humans who lived near the magic, if they felt more awake and alive elsewhere, that was the price that must be paid.

The king was one of those who left. He went to a tourney and sent word that he would be a few days, and then a few more days, and then he stopped sending word. Perhaps he had nothing to say, or perhaps there were no longer messengers to carry it. Perhaps he had decided that the castle was worth no more of his life.

Toadling never saw him again. She thought of Master Gourami, telling her that her father's house had need of her. She had failed in that, too. Her father's house had dissolved quietly, without fuss, and no longer had need of anything at all.

You don't know that. He could have gone away and taken his blood with him and sired another child or whatever it was that the goddess wanted him alive to do.

This felt too much like an excuse, and Toadling was suspicious of it. More likely, the only choices for her father's house had been a quiet, peaceful ending or a prolonged horror under Fayette. It had needed Toadling to put it out of its misery, nothing more.

And most *likely, I have simply failed, that is all.*

The queen committed suicide one afternoon. She took enough poppy milk to stop a horse's heart and lay down in her bed. She left no note. Perhaps she had expected Toadling to save her again, had hoped to sleep beside Fayette and wake when her daughter's curse was broken. But she died instead, and Toadling took on human form and helped the cellarer and the gardener and the last stablehand to bury her.

"Should we be burying her in holy ground?" asked the stablehand softly, looking at the tiny graveyard and the queen in her shroud. "She didn't die shriven, and they say . . ."

"I don't care what they say," said the gardener. "This is where I'm digging the hole."

Toadling patted the stablehand's arm and said, as gently as she could, "I don't really think it matters anymore."

They put the earth over the queen's face. Toadling stood and watched. It made no sense to her, that the queen with so much useless strength had simply given up. Perhaps she had come to the end of being strong.

Toadling tried to feel something, because her mother was dead, but all she could think of was the Eldest and Duckwight and the others. Were they still alive? It had been many years in Faerie. Millennia, perhaps.

No, they are greenteeth. They are nearly immortal if nothing kills them. Surely their bellies are full and their teeth are sharp.

The queen vanished under a layer of earth. They stood, and finally Toadling said the Lord's Prayer, because she could not think of anything else to do. The others joined in, tongues stumbling over the words, and the cellarer only muttered, "Amen," at the end and nodded.

And that was the end. The stablehand and the cellarer waited while the gardener went about, unhurried, harvesting the last seed heads from the plants and stuffing them into her pockets. Then they all left together. The stablehand began to sing when the shadow of the keep fell behind him, in a deep baritone, and the cellarer joined in, and only the gardener looked back once at Toadling.

And then she was alone with the birds and the brambles and the changeling in the tower and the wagtails on the grass.

Halim listened to her story with the fire popping and crackling between them. It was dark and she could only see orange washes of light over his skin and the backs of his hands as he fed branches to the fire.

"And you grew the brambles up after they left," he said.

"I did."

"And she's still there."

Toadling sighed. "The beautiful maiden in the tower," she said glumly. "Although she looks about eight years old, so even if a knight had broken in, they'd be somewhat disappointed. And then I suppose they'd be dead not too long after that."

"You think she'd kill them?" asked Halim.

"I think she'd kill everything if she could. The whole world. And who's going to suspect a child? At least at first?" Toadling wiped her hands across her face.

"And you've been watching over her for two hundred years. More than two hundred years."

"I came to stop her from doing harm. The words of my gift or the terms of my sentence—take your pick."

Halim nodded slowly, almost to himself.

"I don't understand," he said finally. "What is a changeling? Why send one? Perhaps this is a question only a human would ask; I don't know."

Toadling sighed. Master Gourami had explained to her, in abstract language, as if they were creatures that had no relation to her. "They are a great wickedness. To us and to themselves, I think. The great houses steal children from each other, or force their vassals to leave their own. They think it's funny, to leave a rival's child in a human crib. And fairy children grow up in a world where metal burns them and the food is dead in their mouths and they see things no one else sees and they know the world should be different than it is."

"Do they all go bad?" asked Halim. "The changelings?"

Toadling shook her head slowly. "I don't know. I tried with Fayette—I did, I swear—but I wasn't good enough. I couldn't make her understand that the world was real."

"The imams say that the djinn can be good or evil, and that many among them have found God's mercy."

He did not mean it as a condemnation, Toadling knew, but she bowed her head anyway. She had failed with Fayette. That the old priest and the nurse and the queen had also failed was small consolation.

"Maybe the world is full of changelings who learned to adapt," she said. "The great fairies don't much care what happens in the real world, so long as it causes mischief for someone. A changeling that lives long enough and learns to come back to Faerie, though . . ." She shook her head.

Halim raised an eyebrow.

"That's why it's funny to them," said Toadling. "The changelings stink of mortals. Their magic is stunted. They're disgraces to the house." She sighed. "Maybe that's why so many go bad. Maybe they know in the cradle that they're trapped. Maybe another changeling could save them, give them a place to belong. I couldn't." The best she could have offered Fayette was to be a creature like Toadling herself, held in affectionate contempt, and that was not a bargain that Fayette would have been willing to make. Fayette had not cared if people feared her or loved her. She had not cared if they thought of her at all. She simply wanted to take them all apart, because she could.

"Could you take her back?" asked Halim. "To the fairy world?"

Toadling shook her head. "I don't know how to get there. It was all bound up in the spell I was supposed to do and it all came out wrong. I thought maybe if I found a kelpie . . . Sometimes they'll help if you catch them in a good mood. They can go back and forth in any stream. But I can't go find one, and no kelpie would come within smelling distance of Fayette."

She poked at the fire with her own stick. The pain of that loss had scabbed over by now, and Halim, it seemed, knew better than to pick at it.

"I know this is hard to believe," said Toadling, when he had been silent for far too long. "I know. I . . . I am very ugly and she will be beautiful and there is no reason that you should believe the fairy instead of the girl. The stories go the other way." She had heard the stories that the people of the keep told each other, tales of fairies stealing children and causing mischief, souring the milk and spoiling the harvest.

After a year or two, when they had forgotten to be afraid of her, they would tell the stories without remembering that she was there.

She did not try to contradict them. What would she say? That a great lord of Faerie would hardly stoop to cursing a cow, that if a fairy was angry—a real one, not her weak, croaking self—they would be more likely to turn the cow into an armored beast that smashed down the walls; or curse the king with a desperate, humiliating passion for the cow; or simply blast cow, keep, and all living things around it into fine gray dust.

"Not all the stories," said Halim. "There is the one of the monster that comes to the knight, and when he gives her everything she asks, she turns to a beautiful lady."

Toadling gave a hoarse laugh that turned into a toad's croak—*harr-uccc-kk!* The sound startled Halim a little, she could tell. "No," she said. "I won't turn into a beautiful lady at the end of this. This is what I look like."

"It's all right," said Halim. "This is what I look like, too. And I think that knight was a king or a prince or something. Um. I'm not going to turn into one of those, either, I'm afraid. I'm well out of the line of succession."

Toadling started to laugh until she thought that she would choke. She wondered what he would think of the Eldest or Duckwight. They would, by his standards, be hideous—and yet she knew in her heart that they were glorious, lovely monsters with their teeth and huge eyes and webbed, grasping hands.

She wondered what Halim would say to them. She could picture him seeing the greenteeth rising from the swamp and cursing . . . and then apologizing.

And then he would probably greet the Eldest and ask, very earnestly, how he should address her, and then apologize again and say his mother had taught him better, and was she a djinn or a marid or some other sort of spirit, and was it rude to ask, and if so, he'd apologize again . . .

"What do you want me to do?" asked Halim. "Tomorrow, I mean."

The question snapped her from her reverie. She knew the answer. She didn't want to say it, but she knew it.

"Can you kill her?" she asked. "I don't mean . . . That's not a request—that's a question. Do you think you could?"

Halim stared into the fire. His face was drawn and unhandsome itself. "I . . . I don't think so," he said finally. "I want to say yes, for you. Because of what you said. But I've killed a few men, and it's bad. And they have to be coming at me with swords, and it's not like—not like that, exactly. It's like we're all screaming and hammering on each other and you just want everyone else to stop screaming and you hope you stop them before they stop you. It's just noise and mud and not thinking. But it's still bad. Afterward, you remember too much of it. And that's men trying to kill me. I don't think I can kill a little girl who's asleep."

"It's all right," said Toadling, stirring. His description had been rather more vivid than, perhaps, he had intended. "I didn't think you could."

Halim looked guilty nonetheless. "I'm sorry."

"I don't think that's something you have to be sorry for. I haven't done it. I've had two hundred years and I haven't."

"Why not?" asked Halim.

"It was easier to be a toad," said Toadling. "I thought perhaps I could, one day, but then I was a toad for a long time, and as long as I was a toad, I didn't have to worry about it. And then no one could get in, so it didn't matter anymore."

"Didn't matter? But you couldn't leave here, could you?"

"No. But I'd made a mess of the gift. I didn't give it to her properly. So it was only right I had to stay."

"You think you had to pay for *two hundred years* for a momentary slip of the tongue?"

Toadling goggled at him. She could feel the words slipping down inside her, into the place under her breastbone. The other words rearranged themselves to make space.

"There's a very high wall," said Halim, "according to the imams, called al-A'raf. Between hell and paradise. And if you haven't been good enough or evil enough to go one place or the other, you live in this wall. But even those people will eventually enter paradise, because God is merciful." He jammed his chin onto his fist and gazed at Toadling. "It seems like you've been stuck in that wall for quite a long time now . . . That's all the theology I've got in me, incidentally, so I hope it's useful."

Toadling sighed. "I would like to climb down from that wall," she admitted.

"Well, then."

"But I can't just leave Fayette here. She won't die, you know. She'll wake up and she'll claw her way out somehow, and then it'll start all over again." She had a sudden image of the wagtails, their necks wrung, their pale feathers scattered across the grass.

Halim nodded. "I believe you," he said.

Toadling wondered if he still would when he had seen Fayette.

They rose the next morning and did not bother with a fire. The mule, disgruntled, aimed a kick at the air. The horse sidestepped and continued quietly eating grass.

The warm, damp magic flooded around Toadling. She stroked her fingers over the stone wall of the tower as if it were an old friend, an ally in a long, terrible battle.

"The door is bricked up," said Halim. Toadling nodded. The mason had done his work well two hundred years ago.

"The windows are all too small," she said. "Except at the top of the tower. I suppose I could throw a rope down from the balcony up there, and you could climb it. Or you could break down the bricks."

"Neither choice is very appealing," said Halim. He looked up the height of the tower, then at the mortar. "Um. Hmm. Let me see . . ."

He went to his bags and took out more tools. The hammer was a small one for setting stakes, not for breaking down doors, but he took it and a horseshoe nail and began chipping mortar out from around the edges of the bricks.

Toadling tried to help. The magic in the tower was all water, and water liked to pull stones apart. She had told it that it was not allowed to do so and it had obeyed, but it had been sullen about it.

She did not have to tell it twice that she had changed her mind. The magic rushed down the stairs, fierce and merry as it ran downhill, and then Toadling was left frantically trying to stop it, telling it that it couldn't all leave the tower, only a little bit, only a small channel diverted, that the main body of the magic had to stay up in the tower and keep Fayette quieted.

Halim tapped with the hammer and half the bricks fell away in front of him.

"No! Oh no, no, no . . ." said Toadling, jamming both hands into the gap, telling the magic to go back, the bricks were *done,* it couldn't just run away into the earth, much as it longed to.

The magic sulked. It had been still and quiet for so long. It wanted to rage like a torrent, pour over things, sweep obstacles away. But it was her friend, and so it turned in its course and settled back in its bed, sullen and quiet once more.

"I take it that didn't go quite as planned," said Halim.

Toadling exhaled, slumping against the side of the doorway. The darkness yawned before her, deep as a well. "I asked the magic to help. It . . . um . . . did. More than I expected."

Halim nodded. His hair was jeweled with droplets of water, and his sleeves were damp where the magic had rushed over him. "I felt something," he admitted. "Like steam." Toadling nodded.

She reached out with all her senses, trying to see if the disruption had woken the sleeper above. It had been terribly foolish to change the magic that had worked for so long. She didn't know what had come over her, except that she had seen Halim struggling and her first instinct was to try to help. *And you would think after all these years trapped in a mortal world that I would have learned not to trust my first instincts . . .*

But the damage, if any, was done. She did not feel any shifting at the top of the tower yet. Perhaps God had been kind.

The remaining bricks were the work of a few moments to knock away. Light touched the bottom floor of the tower for the first time in two centuries.

"Don't step there," said Toadling, pointing to a dark blotch on the stones.

Halim looked at it, then up at her. "The nurse?" he said. She nodded. He touched his hand to his lips and gave the stain a wide berth.

Toadling squared her shoulders and walked up the tower steps with the knight close behind her.

At the top of the stairs, she paused. The carpets had rotted away, but dead leaves made a slick layer over the stones.

The water magic kept them wet, and small weeds had sprouted in the circle of light from the balcony.

Fayette lay on the bed, bright as mushrooms in the dark. Her skin was white to the point of translucency, and her hair fanned out around her. It had grown in her sleep, but only a little, enough to slide down over her shoulders in a golden curtain. Her dress had faded and was spotted with mold, the hems beginning to dissolve, so that she looked as if she were growing out of the bedclothes herself.

The magic was still rippling and sloshing from side to side, agitated. Toadling clutched at the doorframe, trying to soothe it.

Halim looked over her shoulder and inhaled sharply. "There *is* a maiden in a tower," he said, almost inaudibly. Toadling nodded. Fayette stirred on the bed of mold and mush, frowning in her sleep.

Halim turned. He did not go into the room, as she had expected, but backed away and sat down on the first stone step.

"I thought I'd know what to do," said Halim, as Toadling sat down on the step beside him. "I thought once I got in here and saw what there was to see . . . I thought I'd know what to do next."

Toadling glanced over at him, surprised.

"I thought you could be lying," he admitted, and then flushed. "No, I don't mean—that came out wrong. I'm sorry. I didn't think you were lying to lie. I said I believed you and I meant it. I still do. But maybe you couldn't speak all the truth, or there was a curse on you, or . . ."

"Or I truly was the wicked fairy," said Toadling gently, "and Fayette was the beautiful maiden trapped in the tower."

His flush deepened. He dropped his head and put his

hands over the back of his neck. "But I still don't know," he mumbled to his feet.

Toadling patted his shoulder. It was still strange to her, touching another living being. She felt the weight of his chain hauberk under the softer surcoat. It made him feel more solid than he really was.

He did not sound solid. He sounded as lost and alone as Toadling.

"If I were a proper knight," he said mournfully, "I should probably strike off your head with my sword and take the girl back to my mother."

"Don't do that!" said Toadling, alarmed. "Your mother sounds kind, and Fayette would— *Please* don't do that!"

He raised his head, a smile tugging at one corner of his mouth. "And striking your head off with a sword?"

Toadling shrugged. "I suppose I'd prefer you didn't."

He snorted. After a moment, he leaned slightly toward her, so that their shoulders touched, and Toadling leaned back, and they sat together on the steps for a little time, with the magic washing over them like the sea.

Finally, Halim sighed and stood up. He walked back into the room and stood looking down at Fayette. Toadling followed him as far as the doorway, with her heart in her throat.

She was restless in her sleep now that there were people here. Her brows furrowed, and she opened her mouth and closed it again. Perhaps a parent might have found that endearing, but Toadling saw only the snapping of teeth.

"All right," said Halim, and turned away. "I do believe you."

Toadling waited for the *but*.

It didn't come.

"I am probably mad or a fool or enchanted," he said. "But if so, it is like no enchantment I have ever heard of, and I already knew I was a fool." He gazed at Toadling with his clear brown eyes. "What do we do now?"

"You . . . you're not going to try to wake her?"

He shook his head. "I believe you," he said again, and the words filled up the hollow space under her breastbone the way that few other words ever had.

"Cold iron," said Toadling. "She never liked it, but everyone thought it was the curse, so they didn't force the issue. Perhaps if we could get more, cover the room in it somehow . . ." She lifted her hands and let them drop.

"We will buy a blacksmith's scrap barrel if that is what it takes," he said gravely. "Or a dozen." He reached out his hand to her, and Toadling felt hope bloom, hot and terrible, inside her chest.

She moved forward to take his hand, and there was a sudden motion from the bed, swift as a striking snake, and Fayette's hand closed over Halim's left wrist like a manacle.

No!" whispered Toadling, seeing the ruin of everything. *No, no, I broke the magic, I shouldn't have disturbed it, I drew off too much magic and agitated the rest and then I brought a mortal up here, it was too much, she's awake, she's awake now . . .*

Halim looked down, surprised, and tried to pull away. Fayette's fingers were white bands over his gloved skin, too small to go all the way around but with a grip as strong as stone.

"Who are you?" demanded Fayette.

"My name is Halim, miss," said Halim, polite as ever. "I did not mean to wake y—"

There was a hard crack as Fayette twisted her hand and snapped his wrist.

Halim did not scream, but he staggered sideways, grunting, his skin going gray in the watery tower light.

Oh God, thought Toadling, *she has grown strong in her sleep. She couldn't have done that before, not with her bare hands . . .*

Fayette dropped him. She had not particularly cared who he was. He cradled his broken wrist against his side, limping away, and clutched for his sword with his good hand.

Toadling tried to pour the magic back over her, tried to quiet her back again, but it was useless. She was dumping water over molten stone and watching it boil away into steam.

"Stop it!" said Fayette, batting at the air around her head. "I feel that! You're trying to put me to sleep again, aren't you?" Her green eyes blazed. "It was you all along! You kept me from doing what I could have done!"

Halim drew his sword awkwardly and held it in front of him, less like a weapon and more like a holy symbol.

"I had to stop you!" said Toadling. "You were making a dead woman walk around! You were hurting people!"

"*So what?!*" screamed Fayette, and struck out at her with magic.

She was clumsy. Sleep had not taught her finesse. That was likely why Toadling stayed upright at all. Fayette's magic was a mailed fist and Toadling was water, sliding out of the way, while the blow went on to powder the stone behind her.

The second blow was better aimed, if no more subtle. Toadling slipped out of the way again, but the force splashed out around her and Halim skidded on the wet leaves and went to his knees.

The motion attracted Fayette's gaze like the eye of a

snake. She struck at him instead, and Toadling had to throw herself between them, pulling recklessly on the magic like a waterfall, spinning the blow and sinking it down into the ground.

I have to get her away from Halim. She'll hammer at him until he dies, just because he's weak.

Fortunately, this was easy. Toadling had spent long years trying to control Fayette's temper. Convincing her to lose it was the easiest thing in the world.

"Yes, I stopped you!" shouted Toadling, and Fayette's head snapped around toward her. "I stopped you because you were a weak, pathetic little child, and you'll always be weak and you'll never get to do what you want!"

Fayette screamed and flung both herself and her magic at Toadling.

She could protect Halim against the magic or she could protect herself against Fayette, and that was no choice at all. The waterfall of magic fell down like a curtain over the knight, and Fayette's hands closed over Toadling's throat.

Well, Toadling thought remarkably clearly, as if she had all the time in the world, *I don't think I'll be able to put her back to sleep anytime soon.*

Fayette's fingers dug into her throat, driving her back across the floor. If her hands had not been so small, Toadling was sure her neck would have been snapped in an instant, but Fayette's body had not aged enough and her hands were still the size of a human child's.

"Enough," hissed the changeling. "*Enough.*"

Toadling could not break the hold. All she could do was pray that Halim had the sense to run when Fayette's back was turned.

He won't run. He's a knight.

Yes, but he said he wasn't a very good one.

Toadling had never prayed for another being's cowardice so intently before.

Step by step, Fayette pushed her toward the balcony. The greenteeth had taught Toadling to hold her breath for many minutes, and so she was able to keep up the wall that held Fayette's magic at bay, but doing so took all her strength.

"You were always stopping me," said Fayette. "I could have brought them in. I could have called them."

What is it? What is she talking about? Toadling's vision began to grow dim, and there was a noise like a crowd roaring in her ears. She beat uselessly at Fayette's head with her hands.

Something hard hit her in the back of the thighs and Fayette began to bend her backward, even though she had to reach up to do it. *What is happening?* thought Toadling, and then, wisely, *Oh, I cannot breathe. It is lack of air . . .*

Toads breathe through their skin. It was reflex, when she could no longer get enough air, to change, and so she did, dropping into toad shape, even as the world went dark.

She heard a man scream and then she fell, but only a little way, and something went by over her head, like a bird flying too close, and then there was only silence and air seeping in through pebbled skin and Halim's hand scooping her up from the balcony railing, the one that Fayette had just fallen over.

CHAPTER 8

I thought you'd gone over," said Halim. "I was trying to reach you and I . . . I slammed into her then. She was unbalanced, but I don't know if I meant her to fall." He swallowed. "I think I probably did." Toadling nodded.

They left the tower and she stood looking down at the body for a long time. She knew that she should feel something, that she was probably doing something wrong again, not feeling as she should, but she did not know what she was supposed to feel. Relief that it was over? Guilt that it had ended this way? But she felt nothing. She did not believe that it had ended, perhaps. It had gone on too long and this was too final and sudden and irrevocable. Her long vigil could not simply *end*.

Could it?

Her first instinct, terrible as it was, had been to try to save Fayette. If she had only been injured, then the gods alone knew what Toadling would have done. But there was no saving this. Fayette's body had broken on the keep's hard ground, and even changelings die of such things.

Toadling knew as soon as she saw the body that it was over. The glamour that had lain over Fayette was gone. She had been a hauntingly beautiful child, but what lay broken on the ground would have been as strange to the humans who raised her as Toadling herself had been. Her fingers had too many joints and her neck was too long and the bloody teeth in her mouth were too many and too sharp. Looking at her, Toadling could make a fair guess as to what fairy clan the changeling had been drawn from, for all the good such knowledge did her.

"When she fell, for a minute, she didn't fall right," said Halim, kneeling on the ground beside her. "That sounds mad, doesn't it? But for a moment, I thought she could fly."

Toadling nodded. Her throat was a mass of bruises and her voice was more of a toad's croak than usual. "She might have," she rasped. "If she'd been older. But she could not yet command the air, and it is . . . was . . . not in her nature to ask."

A little longer, and perhaps she would have learned. Or she would have learned to command other things instead . . . She remembered Fayette talking about calling *them* in and shuddered. There were worse worlds than Faerie.

Halim rose, wincing a little, and she remembered that his left wrist was broken. "Your arm! You must be in so much pain . . . Let me do something—"

He smiled, but he was a little white around the lips nonetheless.

She moved him farther away from the shattered body. The air seemed a little clearer, the farther away they went. Toadling had a notion that a wound bandaged inside the keep might take longer to heal than one treated outside it, and she did not examine that belief too closely but led him outside the thorn hedge to his campsite.

It was an easy enough wound to treat. The break had been swift and clean, and Halim knew enough battlefield medicine that, between them, they were able to set it. Toadling made a poultice of dock to draw the swelling out and placed rowan twigs along the splint to draw the malice out.

"Good enough," he said, moving his fingers and wincing. "I'll have a fine ache when the weather changes, but I'll hold a shield again." He smiled crookedly. "It will make attending to certain needs difficult, I grant you, but God will forgive my clumsiness until it heals."

"I'm sorry," she said, head bowed over his arm. "I'm sorry."

"*You* didn't break my arm."

"No, but . . . if I had done something . . . been better . . . if we could have stopped her sooner . . ."

His eyes were grave. "Some things can't be fixed."

"We couldn't change her," said Toadling, feeling as if the words were broken glass in her ruined throat. "The queen loved her and the nurse and I tried for years and love wasn't enough and trying wasn't enough and nothing we did changed *anything*!" She let out a croaking sob. Halim gathered her up awkwardly in his arms and she gripped the edges of his surcoat and cried black ink tears onto his shoulder. "It should have mattered. All that love and all that trying should have changed . . . *something* . . ."

"I know," he said. "I know."

Toadling shuddered and shivered against him. She wanted to turn into her quietest, coldest toad shape and sink into the mud and not think for a long time. But she stayed human instead, and Halim held her the way that no one had held her since she had left the greenteeth behind.

Eventually she ran out of tears. There were centuries' worth still locked up inside her, but her body could only shed so many at a time. She was aware that her eyes were ringed with black and looked as if she had been beaten, but there was nothing to be done about that.

"I'm sorry," she said again. "I'm sobbing all over you when I should be mixing up a draft for your pain."

"You were in pain as well," he said, "and bones heal faster than spirits, I think. But I've felt a great deal better than I do now—I won't deny it." And then he kissed her forehead.

Toadling had no idea what to do about that, and apparently neither did he, because he released her and went to lead his horse back, one-handed, to the fire.

The herbs in the keep's garden had run wild over the years and many had died completely, strangled by their stronger relatives. Toadling had to make up the difference with magic as best she could, and magic was always chancy.

Her magic was indeed coming back to her, though. She could feel it landing on her skin in drops, each one sinking in, a little more and a little more, like rain falling on a parched land. Much of the strength in the tower had not been her own but a gift of water, and that she let go, to run back into the earth and fill the wells that had gone dry two hundred years before.

She handed him the draft in the little cup that had held holy water (was it only a few days earlier? It seemed a lifetime), and he drank it down without hesitation, as if he trusted her. *Well, it would be ridiculous to poison him now, after everything . . .*

She built up the fire awkwardly. There was too much water clinging to her still and it was inclined to smoke and steam sullenly. The mule laid his ears back and made an ill-tempered noise as the smoke drifted over them. But eventually it quieted and began to behave as a fire should, and Halim sat gazing into it and nodding off.

Toadling helped him, only half-conscious, into his bed-roll. He smiled up at her and the place on her forehead throbbed like a brand where he had kissed her. It felt isolated from the rest of her flesh, as if with that kiss, the mortal world had reached out to claim her, the way that the semicircle of scars on her palm had claimed her for Faerie.

She sighed. There was still fairy work to be done. The body could not be left to poison the air around it. After that . . . well. After that, the world was open. She could leave. She could go with Halim. She could go elsewhere, find a kelpie, and be swept down under the water and into the fairy realm. She had so many choices and she had never had choices, never been given a chance to choose anything more important than what fish to snatch or what herb to pick.

It was paralyzing. *How does anyone manage? There are too many streams and they all flow and all of them could be good and there's no way to know. How does anyone ever choose to do anything?*

Well. No matter what choices she did or did not make, there was still a task remaining. Toadling rose to her feet and walked through the hacked corridor in the thorns.

Fayette's body lay white as bone in the moonlight. Someone familiar with death might have noticed already that there was something swift and not-quite-right about the way that it was decaying, just as there had always been something swift and not-quite-right about Fayette's life. The hollows of her hair had turned dark brown and black, like dead leaves, and her eyes had gone black and hard as stones.

"I'm sorry," said Toadling, to Fayette or the queen or the dead nurse or all the creatures that the changeling child had tormented. It was useless, but she was the last one standing, so perhaps that was her task, to apologize to all the others. "I'm so sorry."

And then, because she could not leave the body to scavengers—God knew what horrors that might unleash, if the carrion crows tasted fairy flesh—she knelt down and made a request of the earth.

Cover her up, she begged the ground. *Let her do no more harm, even in death. Please.*

Water she could command, but earth she could only ask. It would not have surprised her if the earth was angry at her for diverting its water away for so many years.

She sat for a long time, because earth does nothing swiftly at first, but slowly, slowly, the ground began to move and loam mounded itself up around the changeling body's fingertips, and grains of earth settled over her hair. Before the moon had crossed more than half the sky, there were mosses spreading a quilt across Fayette's deathbed, and the last strands of gold had vanished underground.

Toadling did her best to help, drawing up water for the mosses, but the earth did most of it. She rose at last, numb with gratitude, and made her way away from the keep for the last time.

The moonlight was silver and the grass dense as fur. Toadling sat by the banked fire, watching the hillside shake itself and become a hare with eyes that held the moon.

Halim slept soundly on the far side of the fire. Toadling thought that he likely would not wake until the goddess chose to let him.

She folded her hands in her lap and waited.

"Well?" said the hare.

"Fayette's dead," said Toadling.

"Hmmph," said the goddess. "Took you long enough."

What?

The great full-moon eyes narrowed to gibbous. "You were sent to stop her from doing harm. The spell would have done as much, in time."

"I was supposed to *kill* her?"

"The dead do no harm to anyone."

Toadling, friend of water, found her mouth had gone bone-dry. "Then why send me? *Anyone* could have killed her—Master Gourami—you—a mortal—"

"And call the wrath of a great lord of elves down on our heads?" said the goddess. "No. But *you* had a right to retake your place. Even they would be forced to agree to that."

Toadling found that she was shaking with unaccustomed rage.

She had been frightened of Fayette. She had been afraid for Halim. But rage was new to her, and she hardly knew what to do with it.

She swallowed it down as if it were swamp water and felt tears pouring down her face, black and venomous.

The goddess watched her, cool and remote. "Did you expect a goddess to be kind?"

"It seems that I should not have," whispered Toadling, wiping at her tears.

"Expect it? No." The goddess shook herself again, and her grass-fur rippled as if wind were bending it against the hill. "We are made of cruelty and kindness both. But we also keep our promises."

"You promised me nothing."

"Not you," said the hare. "But I made an oath to the Eldest of Greenteeth."

Toadling looked up. Her heart had leapt, like a hare itself.

"Will you take me home?"

"Climb up on my back," said the hare, and she did.

The passage to Faerie took no time at all. The goddess ran, and from one step to the next, they passed out of the mortal world. Toadling felt magic roll over her like the tide, half-sweet, half-salt, and she let out a gasp and laughed and sobbed into the goddess's silver fur.

They came to a stream overhung with branches, where waterweed grew thick among the stones. Toadling did not remember getting down from the goddess's back and did not see her leave. She saw only the water.

She fell into it, scrambling over the stones to the deeper channel. Her skin sang with the touch and she plunged her head under the surface, gulping it through her damaged throat, and let out a squalling cry that echoed along the riverbed.

It never occurred to her to doubt her welcome. Such was the gift of a child raised with love.

Reedbones came first, but she had always been the fastest. She wrapped her long, bony arms around Toadling and squalled and chuckled, stroking her hair with webbed fingers. The others arrived by ones and by twos. Duckwight pulled her away from Reedbones and held her so close that Toadling could feel her hard green heart beating inside her chest.

And then, at last, the Eldest. Ageless still, with her necklace of holed stones and her teeth like sabers and fingers that could snatch a man from a riverbank and wrap twice around his neck. Snails and water bugs lived in her hair, and she was so beautiful and so glorious that Toadling's black tears mixed with black water as the Eldest lifted her up and croaked, "Welcome home, beloved."

EPILOGUE

It was a long time later, or not very long at all. The flow of time depended on which world you stood in. Toadling slept in the crook of the Eldest's arm, her lips above the water, tangled in the greenteeth's waterweed hair.

Her sleep was troubled. There was a knight in it. He was not handsome, but he had kind eyes, and he apologized when he swore. He was very fond of his mother, and he had thought it was rude to throw moly and salt into a toad-girl's face. The skin on her forehead pulsed with the memory.

She thought, *I am home now. I do not need to remember.*

Duckwight caught fish with her the next morning. They tickled them out of the water together, then bit them behind the eye to kill them. Two kelpies stormed by on the riverbank, their muscles moving under their skin. The lead one tossed his head, prancing, and Duckwight shrieked something appreciative and obscene.

I am not beautiful, thought Toadling, and Halim's memory answered, *No. But you are interesting. And sad.*

"You're troubled," said the Eldest, rubbing her clawed fingers over the silver scar on Toadling's palm and then, thoughtfully, across Toadling's forehead, where the kiss still lingered against her skin.

"There was someone in the mortal world who helped me. I left without telling him goodbye."

"Was it important to tell him?"

Toadling stared at her fingers, at the little webs at the base. Was it? Did it matter? He was mortal and Toadling was . . . something else. Something betwixt and between. Something less, not more. She had no family, no people, and the little that she knew of the mortal world was two centuries out of date. She might be no more than a burden to him.

And yet . . . and yet . . .

He likes stories. And I know so many. And he says his mother is kind.

"Yes," she said. "I think it was."

"Then you must go back," said the Eldest, as if it were the easiest thing in the world.

"What? But what if . . . what if I stay a little longer? He wanted me to meet his mother and maybe a Benedictine monk and a rabbi . . ."

The old monster's eyes lidded over as she smiled. "You'll outlive him," she said. "By a thousand years. We'll be here afterward. We'll always be here. You're ours and we're yours."

She gathered Toadling up in her arms and sang her a lullaby of fish sleeping in the depths of the stream and the hands that snatched them from the mud.

Duckwight cried a little again. Duckwight always cried. Fadeweed said nothing but pressed a fish into Toadling's hands.

The kelpies came snorting and trotting out of the water, dangerous and strong. Toadling swung herself up on one's back and he plunged back into the water, down into the whirling depths of the lake. She clung with her legs and felt the water horse's muscles pulse as he thrust himself between worlds.

It had been nearly two seasons in Faerie. In the mortal world, the moon was sinking and the air was turning pre-dawn gray.

A ride on kelpie-back was not as gentle as a ride on a hare with full-moon eyes. Toadling clung with all her strength. He splashed through streams, and the taste of the water told her where she was, so that she could call directions to him and watch his small black ears flick back to catch them. Then he would run, faster than any mortal horse, swift as floodwater rising.

Just as the sun touched the edge of the sky, the kelpie stopped. Toadling slipped down, gracelessly, before he could buck her off. Kelpies found that sort of thing amusing.

He snorted at her. His breath tasted like the last gasp of a drowning man, and his eyes glinted with blood-black shadows.

"Thank you," said Toadling.

"Call if you need me," he said, curling his lips back from his teeth. "Maybe I'll come. Maybe I'll drown you."

"You can't drown me," said Toadling, amused.

"Then I'll take you home instead."

She nodded.

He whirled and ran back over the grass. His hooves left puddles filled with swirling water behind him.

Toadling took a deep breath of mortal air. Yes. One day she'd call him and go home.

For now, though, she walked over the crest of the hill, toward the cold campfire, where Halim was just beginning to wake.

Acknowledgments

Way back when, in 2015, in my other life as a children's book author, I had a book published called *Harriet the Invincible,* the first of the Hamster Princess series. Harriet, the hero, is very fierce and very confident, and she's also the princess at the heart of a "Sleeping Beauty" retelling (also a hamster). It was a fun romp and I enjoyed writing it enormously, and a lot of readers liked it, too.

But as inevitably happens when you retell a fairy tale—or at least when I retell one—I found myself with all these extra possibilities in my brain afterward. Directions that I could have gone but didn't. Characters that I could have written but passed over in favor of others. Themes that went unexplored, ideas that never got fleshed out, all the usual writing baggage. And yet somehow, this time, it was different. It didn't go away.

Apparently, I was not quite done with "Sleeping Beauty," or perhaps the story wasn't quite done with me.

I usually find my way through a fairy tale by questioning all the assumptions in it, starting with who the hero and the villain are. The wicked fairy that curses Sleeping Beauty is supposed to be the villain, of course. (And yes, I did love the movie *Maleficent,* but even then, the princess is one of the good guys.) So in this case, I started thinking, what if the princess was the villain? After all, why would you trap someone inside a hedge of thorns, anyway? Because you wanted to contain her. Because there was some reason you didn't want her to get out. Because she was dangerous, and maybe you weren't a very skilled fairy, so you did the only thing that you could think of to do.

I wrote about three paragraphs with this idea in mind, and Toadling more or less dropped into my lap, fully formed. I rapidly found myself writing the diametric opposite of the book that I had just written. (It's hard to think of two characters less alike than Toadling and Harriet, although I love them both.)

Once I had Toadling, the whole thing just flowed. It's lovely when that happens. (Also, sadly, rare.) Many characters bolt off with the story, and I am left staggering behind them, frantically trying to take notes, but Toadling was very polite. Her backstory unfolded pretty much as I typed it. I learned she was raised by greenteeth as I wrote the sentence about them; I learned that she could turn into a toad when she did it on the page—all the little discoveries that you always make writing a book, of course, but happening at my usual typing speed, without sitting and staring at the wall for an hour, or nearly rupturing my wrist tendons trying to keep up.

It was really very sweet, and so if someone asked me about *Thornhedge,* I would probably say that it is a sweet book, and then presumably someone would point out that the heroine is raised by child-eating fish monsters and the villain is torturing people and animating the dead, and I would be left flailing my hands around and saying, "But it's sweet! Really!" because I am not always the best at judging the tone of my own work.

. . . I still think it's sweet, dammit.

The other amusing thing about *Thornhedge* is that it was the first book I sold to Tor, though it has come out after a couple of others, because publishing. I had written most of it, had it lying around in my mental trunk, and wasn't sure what to do with it. Novellas were hard to place at the time. There was one magazine that told me flat out that they couldn't afford to pay me anything like what it was worth, which I respected, but which left me with this weird wrong-length . . . thingy.

And then I saw that Tor had an open submission period for novellas coming up.

Huh, I thought. *I should send this in. When is that, again?*

Then, a few minutes later: *Waaaaait a minute—I have an agent! Agents don't have to wait for that! They can just send in books!*

(I have written more than forty books now, and I am still sometimes not entirely clear on this whole "being a professional writer" gig.)

So my agent sent in *Thornhedge,* and Tor very kindly came back and said, "Yes, we will take this, and also, what else you got?" which is why *Nettle & Bone* and *What Moves the Dead* have also come out by the time you're reading this. So I am very grateful to them for taking the chance, and also to Toadling, weird as it is to be grateful to a figment of your imagination, for paving the way.

Further thanks go to our awesome sensitivity readers, Heba Elsherief and Sanaa Ali-Virani, who improved my portrayal of Halim to no end and cheered him on his adventure; and to my editor, Lindsey Hall, who I choose to believe defeated multiple other editors in a no-holds-barred cage match to champion *Thornhedge.* And of course, to my agent, Helen, who said that yes, I did indeed have an agent, and sending in manuscripts was indeed what she did. She is very patient with me, including the time that I had to get off a call because a penguin was trying to eat my shoelaces.

Finally, to my beloved husband, Kevin, who always has to read these at about the 60 percent mark so that he can reassure me that it does not shame my ancestors, and who makes sure that I do not live on frozen food and dry pasta when in the throes of creation.

All of you are wonderful, and I would write many fewer books if I had to try to flounder along without you. Thank you.

T. Kingfisher
North Carolina
June 2022